Luiz Calado

Andy Comins

About the Authors

FRANCESCA LIA BLOCK (left) is the author of the *Los Angeles Times* bestsellers *Guarding the Moon, The Rose and the Beast, Violet & Claire,* and *Dangerous Angels: The Weetzie Bat Books,* as well as *Necklace of Kisses* and many other books. She lives in Los Angeles.

CARMEN STATON lives in Los Angeles with her family. She is working on *Dreamstone,* a book for children.

ruby

ruby

a novel

francesca lia block

carmen staton

HARPER

NEW YORK • LONDON • TORONTO • SYDNEY

HARPER

A hardcover edition of this book was published in 2006 by
HarperCollins Publishers.

HarperCollins books may be purchased for educational,
business, or sales promotional use. For information please
write: Special Markets Department, HarperCollins Publishers,
10 East 53rd Street, New York, NY 10022.

FIRST HARPER PAPERBACK PUBISHED 2007.

Designed by Renata Di Biase

The Library of Congress has catalogued the hardcover
edition as follows:

Block, Francesca Lia.
  Ruby : a novel / Francesca Lia Block and Carmen
Staton.—1st ed.
    p. cm.
  ISBN-13: 978-0-06-084057-0
  ISBN-10: 0-06-084057-9
1. Abused children—Fiction. 2. Domestic fiction. I. Staton,
Carmen. II. Title.
813'.54—dc22

                                            2005056394

ISBN: 978-0-06-084058-7 (pbk.)
ISBN-10: 0-06-084058-7 (pbk.)

07 08 09 10 11 ❖/RRD 10 9 8 7 6 5 4 3 2 1

for our children

acknowledgments

We would like to thank our families and friends and everyone at HarperCollins, especially Alison Callahan.

ruby
◊

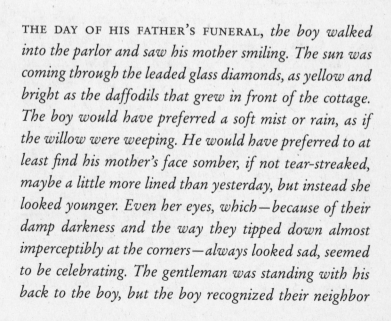

THE DAY OF HIS FATHER'S FUNERAL, *the boy walked into the parlor and saw his mother smiling. The sun was coming through the leaded glass diamonds, as yellow and bright as the daffodils that grew in front of the cottage. The boy would have preferred a soft mist or rain, as if the willow were weeping. He would have preferred to at least find his mother's face somber, if not tear-streaked, maybe a little more lined than yesterday, but instead she looked younger. Even her eyes, which—because of their damp darkness and the way they tipped down almost imperceptibly at the corners—always looked sad, seemed to be celebrating. The gentleman was standing with his back to the boy, but the boy recognized their neighbor*

by his broad shoulders, long legs, and dark, tousled hair. From the back, when you couldn't see his spectacles and refined features, he resembled an athlete more than a scholar. For the first time it struck the boy that his mother and this man looked a little like brother and sister. It had something to do with their long eyelashes and full mouths as well as their coloring.

The man had his hand on the small of the boy's mother's back.

The boy thought of his father laid out in a casket. He looked nothing like him and their natures were so different. The boy was like his mother, always pretending he was someone else, somewhere else, believing there was a ghost in the well and a sprite living in the forest at the edge of town. The ghost was evil but his mother assured him it could not get out. She'd tried a number of spells but it was still there, muttering about catching the winged forest creature and feeding it to the tabby cat. The sprite was a redhead, kindhearted and graceful. The boy had fallen asleep in the wood once and been awakened by her dancing on his forehead, like a spider. His mother promised him that the sprite would find a way to charm the tabby. She was good with animals and knew their ways.

The boy's father hated when they talked about things

that weren't real, things you couldn't prove with science.

"I don't want you getting ideas into his head," he told his wife. "He's flighty enough as it is."

So the boy had tried to record the ghost's voice and photograph the sprite but, of course, neither of them chose to reveal themselves for the purpose of convincing an unbeliever. The tape came back garbled, as if rain was falling into the well, although it was a cloudless day, and the photos were grainy, with splotches of colored lights here and there. The boy's father remained unconvinced.

In spite of their differences, though, the boy loved his father. He was, after all, his. He had come home from work every day and sat at the table with them and kissed his son good night on the forehead every evening. He had taught him science and history and discussed politics with him. He was a good man, hardworking, faithful, honest.

The boy knew his mother was lonely. She and his father slept in separate rooms, and sometimes the boy heard her voice whispering late into the night, reciting the spells his father forbade, and sniffing back tears. Still, it did not seem right that she should be smiling so soon.

When she glanced over the man's black-clad shoulder, she saw her son's face and the smile was gone.

This is what the boy would remember. Not only that she was smiling but that she stopped when she saw him, as if it were wrong.

On the day of his father's funeral, the boy wished for mist.

the island of the animals

MY FIRST MEMORY

I am three years old. I want Opal to play with me but she doesn't want to. I keep going to her bedroom, pestering her mercilessly, but she won't listen. So I go to the den in the basement, where my parents are watching television. The only light is from the TV screen. There are no windows down here. The air smells dusty. My sister has followed me.

Eighteen years later, and here, in my mind, it is all still happening.

My father leaps over the back of the couch and grabs Opal by her hair.

He punches her in the face.

My mother jumps on my father, screaming and hitting him, trying to pry his hands off Opal's throat. He knocks my mom into the wall. A chair topples over. He is still strangling my sister. I can see her pinned to the ground. I can see her eyes.

I don't remember why he stops. He just stops. He lies calmly back down on the couch and orders my sister to go play with me. She is still on the floor, sobbing. I can hear the pressure of his fingers in the sound of her voice.

I am watching all of this, standing right here, filled with rage and disgust, but also completely separate. Then a rushing, sucking sensation, as if my soul has just dropped down into my body for the first time.

And now I know who I am.

I am Ruby. I am three. I have decided. I will fight back.

DURING MY CHILDHOOD, I had what my mother called a wild imagination. My father called me a liar. Ironic, isn't it, coming from him. What I was—I was a survivor.

IN THE MIDDLE OF THE LAKE there was a small island. I took my boat there every day. An old white mare carried me through the woods where each tree held a small wooden house supported and concealed in its branches. The air was decked with the scent of flowers I'd never seen before. Their fragrance was almost visible; it made my head spin.

We came to a large mansion. It was like some kind of plantation home, white with black shutters, columns, a wraparound porch with big rocking chairs and wooden palm-leaf fans. Quirky contraptions for using the natural energy of the sun and wind. All the plants in the overgrown garden had healing properties if you knew how to use them. Inside the house, the animals roamed free. They had been rescued from their abusive homes. A parrot with its eyeball burned out by a cigarette butt. An ocelot that had been declawed and whipped until it could barely walk. Lizards smuggled from their native habitats, crammed together inside of tiny boxes so that their frills had broken off. I spent the day with the animals. They sat on my shoulders and in my lap. I fed them berries and sang to them. I never wanted to leave.

But back I went to sit at my parents' table, watching my father clenching his cigarette, dropping ashes on the linen.

Once, my fingers got in the way. When he burned me with the cigarette he insisted it was accidental.

At least I was safe in my mind, though. I knew the animals were waiting for me.

. . .

THERE WAS A BOG behind my friend Amy's house. I spent hours there, feeling the squishy earth between my toes, lying on my stomach near the water's edge watching the toads mate and lay their eggs. The males mounted the females, who expelled eggs into the mud. Then the toads all left. The eggs hatched into tadpoles, and I dropped peat moss onto the water's surface to see the frenzied black squiggles feed.

Over the spring, I watched them grow legs, become toads, too. My own private lesson in evolution.

Sometimes, at twilight, I saw bright, eerie sparks just beneath the shallow marsh water. Eyes. The creatures were slicked with mud and they spoke in soft, guttural whispers. I wondered, would they evolve, become girls like me, or were they what I would become if I chose never to leave?

"They know all about us," I said, watching my father swallow his meat at the opposite end of the long table. We were the only ones there.

"Eat your food, Ruby."

"Make me."

He scraped his chair back and left the room. I sat waiting, motionless, gripping my knife. When he came back, he was holding a yardstick. He reached out and, very slowly, tapped me on the top of the head with the end of the stick.

I ALWAYS LOVED TREES. I couldn't stop touching them. Sometimes I rubbed my hands with the residue from their leaves and sniffed my fingers to calm myself as I fell asleep at night. I started climbing as soon as I was tall enough to reach the lowest branches. And there was one tree I loved most of all.

He was old and strong. Large, low branches spread out like a cupped hand with the fingers open. I could climb halfway to the top and not worry that my weight was too much for him. We talked many times, until we could understand each other's words. Old man tree. He said that not all trees are men, only a few, most are women. He told me how the years had passed for him, not years like ours, just passages of time based on growth and weather. I never fully understood the system but I listened, and I told him my secrets. I told him about the one hundred books I'd read that summer, running back and forth to the library to win the local contest. I told him the stories I'd made up.

"What's the difference?" he asked.

"Between what?"

"The man beating the child. The woman in the sky

who makes a man from the pieces of her body she loses each night."

"One is real. One is fantasy."

"But what's the difference? What does that mean?"

I couldn't explain, because the lines were blurry for me, too.

For example:

I am at my grandparents' farmhouse, sitting on the floor, playing with my plastic farm animal set while everyone is watching TV.

"Where are King and Queen?" I ask.

My mother looks at me sideways, her eyes large and her mouth small.

"What did she say?" my father barks.

"She asked where King and Queen are," says my grandmother.

Everyone stares at me. Even my grandfather stops watching the television screen. My mother rubs her arms to smooth out the goose bumps.

"What do you mean, Ruby?" she asks. "Are you playing a game with your toys?"

"No," I say. "King and Queen. The dogs."

The German shepherd and the collie. That morning, we went walking on the hill beside the house. Under the big, old walnut tree. They were on either side of me. It was very sunny and I was wearing a delicate pale yellow dress.

"How could you know that?"

"How could she know about that?"

"She must have heard us talking."

"She must have seen photos."

"She's never seen photos."

My mother explains that King and Queen died a long time ago. I never saw them.

I insist on it. They say it's impossible. I know it is true. Or:

I am seven years old. Very ill. Mom and Dad are fighting about taking me to the doctor. He doesn't want to. I can't eat and can barely drink. Losing weight. High fever. Can't walk. I crawl to the bathroom to throw up the Popsicle I just ate.

That night, I am asleep on the floor of the bathroom and then I am hovering—weightless, warm, full of light, looking down at my small body huddled on the cold tile. I am flying through the house, feeling a fresh breeze on my face, looking down at everything with love. My books and toys, my mother asleep in front of the television, her face in the strange light, the carpet with the red roses, the china with the blue bearded iris pattern, the yellow kitchen that still smells of the bread my mother baked that morning, my sister, Opal, asleep in her room at the far end of the house. Why is her room so far away? I wonder. I can see why they named her Opal. Her skin is so milky and luminous it is almost blue.

Time to go back.

No. Why? I don't want to go back.

It is time.

The next morning, Dad takes me to the hospital. I am lying in the room with Dr. Martin, who is looking at my X ray, telling my father they don't know what is wrong with me. They don't think I'm conscious.

"I know what those are," I say, sitting up. I am pointing at the large bubble shapes all over my torso in the X ray.

The doctor looks at me, surprised. "What do you think they are, Ruby?"

"Giant gas bubbles."

He examines the dark death-mask image again. "You're right. How did you know that, sweetie?"

"I don't know. I just did," I say. "Maybe I figured it out when I left my body. I was looking down on everything and I understood things."

Dr. Martin comes and sits beside me. He takes my hand. I am aware of my father in the room, watching us. He has never held my hand or called me "sweetie" this way. He almost never calls me anything. It was my mother who named me and my sister—her precious gems.

The doctor does not address my father, as you might expect, instructing him in my care. He speaks directly to me instead, as if he senses that I am the one who is going to deal with this, make myself better.

"You have to eat, Ruby," he says. "Even if it makes you feel sick. And someday maybe you can come back here and work for me. You seem to know a lot for a little girl."

"She knows a lot," my father mutters when we are driving home. "A lot about lying."

But it wasn't lying. I don't know what it was. My imagination? Real?

SO I COULDN'T EXPLAIN to my old man tree about the difference between reality and fantasy. I didn't know.

We had to move away from my tree. I was too sad to say good-bye to him. I've always felt guilty for that. He was the first man I trusted.

UNTIL STEVEN.

My friend Amy had come to visit us in the new town. We went cruising the square in her mother's station wagon. Everyone knew each other, so a new face stood out and Amy was very pretty.

"Hot," Steven would say later. "It's cool she looked so hot because otherwise you and I never would have met."

A boy in a Camaro flashed his lights at us, the signal to pull over, and we did. He had short, dark hair, broad shoulders. He was interested in Amy but they didn't have much to say to each other, so he and I started talking.

I knew how to talk to boys. You look them in the eye. You listen carefully. You ask questions. You act casual, not girly, like a friend. But sometimes you reach out, almost imperceptibly, and touch their sleeve, their wrist. It is important to not only touch the cloth but to make contact with actual skin.

Steven took me out the next weekend. Amy had gone back home and I was lonely. I remember how good it felt to walk out the door of my father's house and get into Steven's car. I was free. I was safe.

After the pizza and the movie we had sex in the back seat. I knew something about that, too. It was such an easy way to escape.

ONE NIGHT, I HEARD STEVEN at the window. I let him in and we lay on my bed, watching *60 Minutes*. There was a segment about a virgin rain forest that had been discovered in Africa. It was possibly the last untouched terrain. The gorillas had never seen a human, so they did not know to be afraid. They came right up to you with long, questioning faces. Only the elephants knew. Their kin had sent the message. *Fear them.* The elephants knew, but when the natives came, the gorillas just stood there until all the adults were killed, just like that, one after the other, and the babies stolen to sell. The dead gorillas were sold, too—their hands and heads to the healers, their fur to wear, their meat to eat. The Western man who had found this place was trying to preserve it. It was perhaps the very last. He had set out to rehabilitate some of the baby gorillas, the ones who had lost their parents. But how would they ever get back where they came from? So as not to die, a primate must bond. If they bonded with the humans who were helping them, they could not be separated.

I was crying and trying to tell Steven about the gorillas and the rain forest, but he just changed the channel to a football game and ignored me.

Later that night, when we were having sex, I moved my mouth to his but he moved away.

"What are you doing?" I asked him.

"What?"

"Why don't you ever kiss me?"

"I kiss you."

"I mean really kiss."

He pulled out and flopped over on his side, his back to me. I got up and sat on a chair with my feet tucked up under my thighs, wondering what I was doing.

I thought I was safe. But, like the gorillas, I had bonded falsely. And now I didn't know how to separate and survive.

SO WE WERE TOGETHER three years. It is hard to imagine that I stayed that long. And in some ways, it isn't. You become what you come from. Unless you refuse.

On the morning of my twentieth birthday, Steven called me. We had plans to go to the one nice restaurant in town that night. We were going to discuss our move to California. Steven would go into real estate. I was going to work as a nanny, get my massage license, and publish my short stories. We would live in a cottage by the ocean, covered with morning-glory vines.

"I have something to tell you."

"Hi, honey. What's up?"

"I can't make it tonight."

"Oh. Okay. Why? Are you feeling okay?"

There was a pause, but not a very long one. "I can't see you anymore, Ruby. I'm seeing someone else."

"What? Why are you telling me this?"

"I can't take all your baggage, Ruby," he said.

states of sound and silence

I HAD VERY LITTLE BAGGAGE when I left. That's what I told myself. A backpack and a tote bag. Not much at all. I saw an ad in the local paper, for a nice Midwestern nanny to take care of two children in Los Angeles. Their grandfather was the doctor who had examined me in the hospital when I was seven. I'd seen him around town since then; I'd babysat for his friends' grandchildren. He hired me on the spot.

Amy and I drove out together. I mostly remember just long expanses of highway and sky, the cornfields turning into mountains, then desert. A feeling of freedom like a landscape spreading out inside of my mind, infinite. But one night we came to a town in Colorado, where the deer hunters were out in full force, wearing the fluorescent orange suits that were supposed to protect them from each other's guns. There was a restaurant with a sign advertising free steaks for the person who shot the biggest stag. My stomach was hurting. We came to a deserted part of the highway and there they were—the deer. They were standing along the roadside, very still, like statues, and they were watching us. I wondered, did they know we were kin, would never hurt them? Were they soul messengers? Or were they just so trusting that they would have done this for any car? Even the ones filled with orange men and their guns?

Amy and I got a motel room with a leaking faucet, mildew, ugly yellow-and-brown bedspreads. We ate our cheese sandwiches, washed out our underwear in the sink, and hung them near the heater to dry for the next day.

Very little baggage. That's what I believed. But that night, I lay awake. There was more baggage than I thought.

IT IS CHRISTMAS EVE. Usual holiday cheer. Dad is in the basement, drinking, listening to country music. Always the basement. He's taken all the phones out and brought them into the basement with him. Before he went down there, he gave Mom the keys to the gun cabinet. Told her she'd better hide them.

Steven is with me in my bedroom. I want him to take me home with him. Instead, he gives me a Maglite flashlight and a phone in case of emergency. He kisses me good-bye and sneaks out. I go to bed wishing for the warmth of his body next to me.

A scream. I am awake.

I'm frozen, can't move my legs. Then I think of my mom, my sister. I force myself out of bed with the flashlight in one hand and the phone in the other. As if these things will protect me. Outside my window the new fallen snow is sparkling in the moonlight. A perfect Christmas scene. The silver-white of sugar cookies, pearl necklaces, angel wings. There are no footprints.

I check on my mom first. She is snoring softly, wearing curlers so she'll be extra pretty for Christmas, alone in the twin bed she has pushed up against my father's twin and covers with one bedspread in the daytime, to make it look as if they still sleep together.

I go downstairs to check on my sister. In this house, too, her bedroom is the farthest away from the others.

On the way to her, I catch a glimpse of someone in a large, framed mirror. Shoulders hunched, eyes burning, mouth grim, hair wild. It can't be me. The creature looks crazy, animal-like, ready to spring. Ready to kill, if you want to know the truth.

Opal is sleeping peacefully, snuggled in her blankets, still holding her teddy bear even though she's a freshman at college. I close her door softly, wishing I could lock it from the inside for her, but there are no locks. My father used to say he was worried about us locking ourselves in by mistake. But that was when we were toddlers, in the first house. He still gets rid of all the locks, every time we move.

I look through the living room, the dining room, the kitchen, the enclosed porch. There's no sign of anyone. No sounds except the clock ticking, the gentle creaks of the wood.

I go back to my room and stay awake the rest of the night, holding Steven's gifts.

THE NEXT DAY, he and my father go hunting together. Steven follows him through the snow. They are both wearing bright orange caps and vests. Steven squints at my father's back and puts his hand on his gun. He is thinking how easy it would be to shoot him, the orange a perfect target.

I THOUGHT I WOULD FEEL LIGHTER, shedding, but, in

every state we drove through after that, I felt heavier with the weight of what I didn't want to believe existed.

In Utah, what I think of mostly is the silence.

One day, we came to a reservation. We drove up to the gate to pay the entrance fee but no one was there. As we stepped out of the car, it was as if we had been sucked into some kind of vacuum. There was no sound. Not a voice, not a car, a bird, a bug. The silence itself was like a thing you could touch.

"I've never been here," I said.

"What?" I heard Amy's voice but it felt far away.

I turned to my right and began walking down a marked path. Along the way were open structures with displays of guns and tools, what the white man had brought to civilize the natives over a hundred years ago. My insides were churning. PLEASE STAY ON PATH, the sign said. I turned and walked off the path down a slope to a large, flat area surrounded by trees. I walked forward and looked to my left, already knowing what I would see. A circle of stones. Nothing grand, just regular river rocks, not huge, just big enough to notice.

"Now I'm going to look up to the right and see a hawk."

There was the bird, making wide, lonely loops in the cloudless blue space.

"Ruby?" I heard Amy's voice, bringing me back.

I started running back to the car, running so hard that my chest hurt.

"What was that?" she asked in the car as I sped away.

"I don't know. I know we can't be here. None of this, this park. It's holy ground. I mean sacred. No one, no white man . . ."

She knew me well enough not to be too freaked out by the things I said. She also knew me well enough to know that I was right—we had to leave.

THERE IS A WOOD behind my parents' house. Sometimes I go there to play. I make tea parties for fairies, using moss-covered tree-stump verandas, acorn cups, bluebell bowls, Queen Anne's lace tablecloths, toadstool chairs and tables. Then I sit and wait for the fairies to come and visit me.

I am here with Opal. We venture deeper into the woods, into a part we have never been before. We are holding hands and we just keep walking, like Hansel and Gretel following the bread crumbs, unable to stop ourselves. Later, we talk about it and say we both had the same sensation of being pulled forward by some dark thing we can't explain.

The trees are thicker here, the light hardly penetrating

the branches. The air smells rich with humus. Our feet sink in the mud. We keep walking. There are no fairy picnics, no tea parties or pixies.

All of a sudden, I stop.

"Here," I say.

"What?" whispers Opal. I can tell she is trembling.

"Something happened," I say. "Something bad happened here."

Like Amy years later, Opal has learned to trust my knowing. And we know enough to leave this place and never come back again, in spite of what pulls us.

We only wish we could follow my knowing inside the walls of our own house.

LAS VEGAS, NEVADA, was the opposite of Utah—all overwhelming sound and light. Fake Egypt, Paris, Rome, New York. The fantasies I saw everywhere had nothing to do with mine. On the way out, we stopped at a roadside casino for dinner. The air was cloudy with smoke and ringing with the sound of slot machines. A Neil Diamond impersonator wearing too much rouge and eyeliner sang on a tiny stage with two barely dressed dancers. I wanted to leave but Amy was starving; the sandwiches we'd brought had run out and we hadn't seen anything but fast food for the last few hours.

Two elderly couples were sitting in a booth in the corner. I smiled at them. You could tell they weren't from these cornfields or mountains or deserts, from these stucco apartment buildings or houses with picket fences and dark basements.

One of the men came over on the way out. He was holding his wife's arm in a gallant way.

"You are a lovely girl," he said to me gently, with a thick Italian accent. "Like a little tomato or a rose with that hair. You should come to Italy. Apollonia? She should come to Italy!"

The woman smiled and nodded. She was wearing an elegant print silk dress and gold jewelry.

"Special thing will happen to you in Europe. You are good luck!"

He blew me a kiss and waltzed off with his wife.

I AM DRIVING IN THE CAR with my father on the way back from a trip to buy cat food.

I am sitting as far away from him as I can. The car stinks from his cigarette butts. My palms feel clammy. Rain drizzles on the windshield. I am wondering why I agreed to come with him at all.

He says, "I have something to tell you."

I tense and keep staring straight ahead at the soft rain.

We'll be home soon, I tell myself. He doesn't even exist, I tell myself. I am Ruby, I tell myself. Like the jewel that is said to open one's heart to love. My mother named me. For the jewel that is said to chase away evil spirits.

"You know," he says, "you hold my life in your hands, girl." His voice is soft but his teeth are clenched. His teeth are always clenched. I keep staring straight ahead, watching the road disappear under the car. We are almost home.

"And I hate you for it," my father says.

WHEN WE ARRIVED IN LOS ANGELES, it was like the walls closing in. Like I couldn't breathe. Everything moving so fast. On our way to the agency in West Los Angeles, Amy and I got lost. We pulled into a gas station, because our tank was almost empty.

A tall, thin man came out of the darkness, moving slowly with his hands up in front of him. He stopped ten feet away from us.

"Now, Missy," he said. "I'm not coming any closer. You need to get that purse off the back of your car and get yourself out of here. This is no place for a couple of little white girls."

He backed away and I managed to thank him before he had disappeared again.

I grabbed my purse, got in the car with Amy, locked the doors, and headed back the way we had come. I wasn't really afraid, though. It's amazing how much more scary the light can be sometimes.

I said to Amy, "Remember Artis Woodbridge?"

"Who?"

"When we were kids. That guy reminds me of him."

Sometimes on my way home from school, Artis Woodbridge would come and meet me by the edge of the meadow. He was a perfectly manicured, elderly gentleman who always wore a vest and a little bow tie. He could identify all the bird songs and plants, and I told him about my day at school. We walked together every day until my father found out. He told me he'd better never catch me with Artis Woodbridge or that would be the end of that. The way he said it made me not want to cross him. It was different when someone else was involved, someone I wanted to protect. He must have spoken to Artis, too, made him feel the same way about my safety, because he wasn't there the next afternoon or the one after that. Once I saw him in town, and he looked at me with such a sad, helpless gaze. I knew he wanted to keep me safe somehow, and he thought staying away was the best thing he could do.

. . .

AMY AND I GOT LOST AGAIN but this time we were too far west, so we decided to keep going to the beach. I had never seen the ocean before. I felt like an alien who had landed on some strange planet. The sun was rising and it was just like some kind of cheesy painting of a sunrise on velvet, almost too beautiful, a wash of colors shimmering in the sky. I wanted to stare right into the ball of flame. It was almost worth going blind just to really see it, brighter than I'd ever imagined, reflected by the water.

In the tide pools at the shore we saw a strange shape moving. We got closer; it was a small octopus.

"Do you think these are here all the time?" Amy asked.

I knelt down in the wet sand. It was red and alien-looking. I wondered what it meant to see one, if there was some symbolism. "I don't think so. I think it's really unusual."

"That makes sense," she said. "I guess I just have to stick with you for the miracles, Ruby."

We found the agency and checked into the motel down the street. We slept all day, and the next morning I met with a lady at the agency for a background check and blood test and all the other paperwork that I'd need to fill out before I could see the Martins.

The agency lady was small and squat and wore an

orange suit. I kept trying not to think of pumpkins. She told me that I needed to wear something conservative but playful to the interview with the Martins.

"There's a Disney store in the mall," she said. "A nice Mickey Mouse tie would do the trick."

So that afternoon Amy and I went shopping. I bought a white button-down shirt, a black pleated skirt, and black Mary Janes at the nearest department store. Then, against my better judgment, I bought a Mickey Mouse tie, just like the pumpkin lady had suggested.

That was what I wore when Amy drove me to the Martins' in Beverly Hills. We sat in her car in front of the sloping lawn, looking up at the large white house with the glassed-in porch and the green trim. I thought of the plantation house on my island. Were there animals inside this one? I knew one thing—if there were, it wouldn't be like at my father's house, where the animals and I would have to protect each other.

Amy grabbed my hand.

"It's huge!" she said.

I nodded. The house was its own little island. I wouldn't mind being stranded there for a while.

I squeezed her hand back, she wished me luck, and I darted out of the car.

Mrs. Martin flowed into the sitting room, wearing

some expensive perfume I didn't recognize and a beautiful lavender-and-black suit. I bowed my head, wanting to apologize for my silly outfit. Pumpkin Lady must have wanted to make sure I looked subservient enough. But Mrs. Martin only smiled at me. She spoke in a thick South Texas drawl.

"Ruby, how nice to finally meet you. Everyone just raves about you. I'm so excited you're here! And the kids, too. That's all Juliet talks about. She and Chase are upstairs now with my assistant, Jennifer. Let me show you around a little while we talk."

While *she* talked; I couldn't get a word in, but I didn't mind. There was something so soothing about Mrs. Martin's voice and her scent and her smile. And the house she was showing me left me speechless, too. It was like a museum. There were English Old Master paintings, ancient pre-Columbian and African sculptures, Chinese cloisonné vases filled with flowers, and walls lined with so many books. But at the same time it was cozy and comfortable, with large, soft chairs and sofas and lots of light flooding through the windows.

The master bedroom was like a tree house—high up, glass all around. You could sit there and feel as if you were right inside the Chinese magnolias and the lemon trees that overlooked the pool.

We got to the room that Mrs. Martin called the nursery, and a little girl came running toward me. She had long, brown braids and big, dark eyes. I got down on my knees beside her.

"Hi, Juliet, I'm Ruby. Who's this?" I pointed to the white toy horse she was holding.

"That's Orion," she said. "He's my sun stallion. Isn't he incredible and also amazing?"

"Most amazing and also incredible," I said. "How old is he?"

"Four. Like me."

Mrs. Martin winked at me. "Juliet loves her horses."

Juliet neighed, whinnied, and began to gallop around the room. It was uncanny how much she sounded and moved like a horse.

"Maybe we'll go riding together," I said.

"Oh, yes, Ruby! That would be so much fun."

Chase was wearing shorts over some kind of leggings with swim shoes, a T-shirt with a lightning bolt on it, an eye mask, and a swimming cap. "Hey, Chase," I said. "How's it going?"

He shrugged.

"Is that a superhero outfit you have on?"

"Chase thinks he is a superhero," said Mrs. Martin.

"I was hoping I'd get to meet a real live superhero

one of these days," I said. "Everyone could use one of them."

Juliet tugged on my arm. "Let's go into the garden for a tea party! Chase can protect us from the scoundrels who try to eat all the cookies."

So we went out into the garden that was dripping with moisture from the sprinklers. I thought about my island again, because I'd never seen most of these flowers before. They were bigger and more exotic than anything in the Midwest, like strange tropical birds. Juliet led me down into a small grotto, where we set out a tea party for Orion and the dolls. Chase played a villain who stole all the cookies and then the hero who returned them to us.

I knew I was here to protect these children and I knew I would make sure they were never hurt. But in some way I knew they were going to protect me, too. From the spirits that had once haunted me. In the Martins' house, I was, for maybe the very first time, completely safe.

THE NEXT DAY, Amy dropped me off again. She had tears in her eyes.

"I'll miss you so much," she said. "Everything will be so different when I see you again."

I leaned over and kissed her cheek. I was crying, too. But not because everything would be different—I wanted that. I knew I'd never see Amy again. And the part of myself that had known her would be gone forever, too.

I AM IN AMY's peach-tiled bathroom with my head back and my mouth open. Amy is sitting in front of me with a bottle. She is dropping silver nitrate onto each of the sores on my tongue. Each drop makes my eyes fill with tears and my body go rigid with pain. Amy got the silver nitrate from her father, who is a dentist. I've had the sores for three days and they are so bad that I can't eat without wanting to scream. Even water hurts. Amy says that this will help, and I trust her. She is one of the only people I trust.

"Oh, Ruby," Amy says, her eyes watering, too.

When the stinging stops, my mouth is immediately better. We go downstairs to have French vanilla ice cream. Nothing has ever tasted so good to me.

"What were those sores from?" Amy asks, serving me another scoop.

"It's stress," I say. "Too much acid. It's why my stomach always hurts."

"But why, Ruby?"

I look at her with everything in my eyes but I don't say a word.

"We've got to get you out of here one day," she says. "As far away as possible."

"THANK YOU," I SAID. "Thank you for keeping your promise."

We kissed each other and I got out of the car and walked up the path to the white house with green shutters.

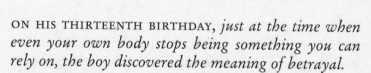

ON HIS THIRTEENTH BIRTHDAY, *just at the time when even your own body stops being something you can rely on, the boy discovered the meaning of betrayal.*

His mother and stepfather had given him a party. They had rented out the pub and even hired a local rock band. His mother told him that she wanted him to feel he could have fun with her in the room. She hoped it would keep him from drinking in the woods and maybe getting some girl pregnant. His mother was happy that she had taught him how to treat a lady, but at the same time she wondered if he was too good at it for someone so youthful. His charm and sensitivity, combined with his faun-like beauty, was a lot to take. On the day of the party, a girl fainted. It might have been from the heat, but the boy's mother believed the girl just couldn't stand the sight of the boy surrounded by so many other adoring females.

Later that night, the boy's mother and stepfather sat with him in front of the fireplace, drinking tea. He thanked them for the party, and his mother ran her fingers through his lush curls, revealing his smooth forehead and slightly arched eyebrows. No wonder the poor child had fainted, she thought. Luckily she had recovered quickly, and the boy had promised his mother that he would call her the next morning to check up on her.

"We have something to tell you, darling," his mother said.

He glanced up. He had been staring into the flames, and for some reason he had imagined he saw his father's face.

His mother and stepfather were sitting close together, watching him with the same expression. The boy couldn't define it. They seemed joyful and sad at the same time, excited and worried.

"We wanted to wait until tonight," his mother said. "Until you were thirteen. It seemed right."

The boy was feeling uncomfortable now. He thought about the lavish party they had given him; it had almost seemed too much. He looked hard into his stepfather's face, studying the shape of his nose and mouth and chin.

That's usually how it is when we hear life-changing news. It's as if we've known it all along and the truth becomes clear just before the words are spoken.

"Just to make it as easy as possible," the boy's stepfather said, "we might as well just say it right out, don't you think?" He looked over at the boy's mother.

She took her son's hand and he squirmed. Something didn't feel right. They could have given him a normal party—a few friends, a cake.

"It's wonderful, really," she said. "I think it will make you very happy when you get used to it."

"What?" the boy glumly mumbled, *as if to say,* Get on with things, will you? *He had, after all, just turned thirteen that day.*

"I'm your real father," the boy's stepfather said, quietly but full of pride, without shame really.

Did this news make the young man happy? He loved his stepfather. His mother loved her new husband. Since the boy's father had died, the house had stayed filled with daffodil light. His parents slept in the same bed. The boy still heard his mother's incantations late in the night but they were of a different kind now. There were no tears.

But it didn't matter. What they told him was still a betrayal. It would still make it hard to trust anything that happened after.

nice men

OPAL AND I USED TO VISIT Bobbi and Marcus Becker, friends of my parents, who owned the florist shop in town. Mr. Becker was also a highly respected veterinarian, who taught at the university. He and his wife lived in a house made of redwood and glass, which they had built themselves way out in the woods. It was filled with art—modern, minimalist Asian, and the Native American pieces Bobbi had inherited from her Blackfoot grandfather. There was a greenhouse off the back, where they grew a lot of the exotic plants for their florist shop. Wild gardens stretched out on all sides, slowly merging with the woods around. Deer came right up to the door to try and eat the day lilies. You'd catch sight of them through the tall windows, munching happily. Mrs. Becker never had the heart to chase them away, so her outdoor garden always had a half-eaten appearance, even though she put up strips of silver foil as a deterrent. Opal and I ate dinner with the Beckers on the screened porch overlooking the woods and a pond with a dock, safe from the mosquitoes that loved to feast on me. After the meal, Opal and Mrs. Becker usually went inside to watch TV or play Scrabble, but I'd stay out there for hours, listening to the night sounds—crickets chirping, bullfrogs croaking, the song of the bobwhite quail, an occasional owl, coyote, or chattering raccoon, and the water of the pond lapping on the dock and the bottom of the two-man metal fishing boat. I imagined I could understand what they were all saying. It was really noisy, like being in a shopping mall where all the little groups are having conversations that create a sort of hum. I was usually alone, and I was grateful for that, just staring up at the moon, lost (or found, really) in her glow. Sometimes Mr. Becker would join me, but I didn't mind. He was the one who taught me to tell apart the night-animal sounds. Once in a while, I'd sit on his lap and let him tuck my hair behind my ears. I never let anyone else do that.

This was my father's friend, I thought. Why couldn't Mr. Becker see who the man really was? But my father was good at deception and I needed kindness in my life.

That was what I got from the Martins, too. Their world was normal. Safe. I was able to just be.

ONE DAY, JULIET AND I were playing with her dollhouse dolls. She handed me the father. He wore a white shirt, brown pants and shoes, and red pullover vest. His face was blank but kind.

"Ruby, do you have a mommy and daddy?" Juliet asked.

I nodded and picked up the mother doll. She was wearing a blue dress and had fluffy yellow hair.

"Do you miss them?"

"I miss my mom, sometimes," I said.

"Tell me about her."

"She has pretty brown hair and teeth like this." I bared my sharp incisors and Juliet shivered happily. "And she is a really good cook. She used to sew me all my Halloween costumes. She had a great-aunt named Ruby and one named Opal and that is how she named me, and my sister, but also because she loves jewels, what they mean."

Juliet nodded solemnly. "What about your daddy?"

I sat quietly for a minute, holding the dolls.

"My father isn't a very nice man," I said.

Juliet looked up at me. Her big, brown eyes were so

sad; for a moment, I wished I hadn't told her. Then she brightened.

"You can share my daddy with me. He's a really nice man," Juliet said.

MY ROOM AT THE MARTINS' was downstairs, off the kitchen. It was very clean and plain. Just my bed and dresser and a closet with a few plain clothes. I didn't go out; I hardly bought a thing. I was saving every penny.

When I had free time, I went into the huge kitchen with one of Mrs. Martin's cookbooks and made meals. French and Indian and Thai and Italian. I'd never really cooked before, but the more I did it, and the more the kids gobbled up the food, the more I wanted to make. Sometimes I'd experiment and come up with my own recipes. I'd use the fresh herbs that grew in the garden and I'd work very slowly, enjoying the feel of the beautiful pots and bowls and knives, closing my eyes to discern the smells.

For exercise, I took Juliet to the stables to ride horses, or I danced. Mr. and Mrs. Martin went salsa dancing every Saturday, and sometimes they gave me lessons. Mrs. Martin would lend me a silk dress and high heels, and we'd put on music and glide around the mirror-lined room with the beautiful wood floors and the ballet barre while Mr. Martin shouted out encouragement.

Mrs. Martin's voice was breathless. "Ruby, you're getting so good, doll, you have to come with us. You'll have the men just going crazy."

But I never took her up on it. I knew I was waiting for something. I just didn't know what yet.

Instead of going out at night, I'd go into the library and choose books and read. Mr. Martin always asked how I was doing and if he could get me anything new. My goal was to read everything on the shelves, to know as much as possible. It was like that summer when I'd run to the library every day, checking out all those books to read and talk about with Old Man Tree. But now it was all right here. I wondered if the books might enter into my consciousness, somehow, while I slept, and fill me with their wonder. Sometimes I read under the big, glossy lemon tree. I wanted to tell her the stories, but she already knew them all.

When I wasn't reading, I watched DVDs. The Martins had a huge collection. A lot of the films were ones that Jack Martin had produced.

One was called *Knights of the Sun*.

I LOOKED UP FROM MY DARK PLACE and there you were. Your smile blooms on your face, sudden and unexpected like a speeded up film of flowers opening. Your eyes shine with something between joy and sadness. Your hair is all reckless brown curls. Your body is lean and fine like a swimmer's. I know what I am waiting for. I know that you are meant to be mine. Why are we given free will if we are not meant to use it? To create. To re-create. I will do whatever it takes.

"WHO IS THIS?" I ASKED Mrs. Martin, showing her your picture on the DVD.

"Ruby, you are so funny!"

"No, I'm serious."

"Don't you see any movies?"

"I didn't much before," I said.

"Ruby is a pure soul," said Mr. Martin.

"That's Orion Woolf," said Mrs. Martin. "He's on his way to being the biggest star in the world, that's what Jack says."

Mr. Martin nodded. "Girls love him. Look at that smile. And he's pretty down-to-earth actually."

"Juliet adores him," said Mrs. Martin. "I have to fast-forward over all the sex and violence so she can see him."

Juliet looked up from where she was putting her horses into their wooden corral. Her eyelashes formed star points as if they were always wet.

"That's who my favorite horsey is named for, Ruby," she said solemnly.

Orion.

I HAD BEEN WITH THE MARTINS for almost a year when Steven called. He had gotten my number from Opal. I'm sure she thought I wouldn't mind; she always liked Steven. I was so shocked to hear his voice that I almost hung up, but then I figured he's harmless, over a thousand miles away, I'm safe here.

He told me about his life and how it wasn't going so well. He had married the girl he had dumped me for. Barb was ten years older than he was. Her dad owned a mechanics shop, so he got a job there instead of going to school like he'd planned. Barb wanted a baby but Steven wasn't ready. She got really angry and upset but all of a sudden her mood just switched. And she wouldn't be home when he got back from work; there were the typical hang-up phone calls. It turned out she was pregnant with his seventeen-year-old cousin's baby.

I couldn't believe the high drama of it all. And I felt so grateful not to be a part of it. But I also felt sorry for him.

When he told me he still loved me, he'd always loved me, I was completely silent. I was afraid if I opened my mouth I'd either scream or vomit. He just kept talking, didn't notice my silence. It had always been like that. He went on to say he had decided he was good-looking enough to try acting or modeling, and he wanted to come to California, just like we'd always dreamed.

"What do you think, Ruby?"

I didn't answer.

"I know you're scared and alone. I'll come and make it all better. I'd bet you'd like that. Can't wait to see you, babe."

Then he hung up.

I just stared at the phone. He wasn't serious, was he? He couldn't be. I knew Steven; he was all talk. And I'm safe, here in the Martins' house, I told myself. He can't find me here among the trees.

But I was wrong. Two weeks later, I was playing with Juliet in the garden room, making a jungle for her wild animals among the ferns, when Jennifer, Mrs. Martin's assistant, came in.

"There's someone here to see you, Ruby. He says he's an old friend."

He was clean-shaven and his hair was slicked back. He had on a La Coste shirt, new jeans, and loafers. Even though he swaggered in and spoke in a loud voice, I could tell he was terrified. It made me feel sorry for him.

"How did you find me?" I asked.

"I got your sister to tell me. I hounded her for months."

I knew Opal wasn't good at saying no. You couldn't blame her, after everything she had been through.

"I can't see you," I said.

"Ruby," he said. "Please. Let me buy you dinner."

"Please leave," I said.

But he came back the next day, and the next. Each time he looked more like a sad puppy dog. Finally, Mrs. Martin stepped in. She told me I had to go.

"You never go out, sweetie. And he's not bad. You could use a little wining and dining."

"What about whining?"

I didn't tell her that Steven broke my heart. It wasn't even really true, anyway. It had been broken long before he came along and now, I told myself, it was whole. I decided to go to dinner with him because I wanted to know for sure how much I had changed.

Steven took me to a large, loud, fish restaurant at the beach. The very tanned waitresses wore Hawaiian-print miniskirts and served fishbowl-sized, fluorescent tropical drinks garnished with skewered canned pineapple and poisonous-looking cherries. I ordered a salad but I didn't feel hungry. Outside the window, the sea and sky and rocks were all the same shade of gray. I wanted to be out there on the water, sailing far away. I remembered the octopus that Amy and I had seen on the beach when we first arrived. I felt like that creature, caught in a tide pool, being examined by Steven's eyes, something unusual and odd, a souvenir he might want to put in a tank and take back home with him.

"I'm sorry, Ruby," Steven said, after he had finished his third beer. "I just want to say I'm really sorry and I will never treat you like that again."

"Again?"

"I want you back. No one else is like you. We can stay out here; you can keep your job. I'm going to get head shots and take acting lessons."

He was talking too fast and I just stared at him. It was like looking at someone reading lines behind a scrim. He was so much less real than you on a DVD.

"I came all the way out here," Steven said.

I shook my head and pushed my plate away. I stared out at the waves crashing on the rocks.

"Ruby?"

"Steven, it is so completely over," I said.

He looked shocked. I realized that he had actually expected me to say yes to him. It made my stomach hurt.

"Did you really think I would want to get back together? My life is different now. I'm looking for different things."

He was angry. I saw it flash in his eyes as though another person were coming up from inside of him, and his teeth were clenched and it made me think of my father. He even pulled a pack of cigarettes out of his pocket and began tapping it on the table. When had he started smoking?

"I know you don't want to be reminded of where you come from but it will always be with you. You can't escape it by pretending it doesn't exist. I was there, Ruby. I saw it."

I remembered, once I was in the basement playing our new video game, sitting at the end of the couch closest to the TV. The TV was always on. My father was lying on the couch, watching me and coaching me. His voice getting louder and louder. I was playing worse and worse the more he yelled.

"You're not trying hard enough!" he screamed.

He started kicking me into the couch. Then he sent me to bed. It was seven at night. I climbed out the window and met Steven.

I had bruises on my legs, and when he asked I told him about them. He took me in his arms and we ended up having sex. But he never said anything. He gave me that flashlight and phone on Christmas but he never said anything. He was right; he had seen what I went through. But he never did anything.

"You can't escape that way," Steven said. "You can't leave where you come from."

He was right. You can't leave.

Unless you do.

It was a little like my first memory, when I was three. Standing there, watching it all. Detaching. Deciding. I could leave.

I got up and threw a twenty onto the tablecloth. Then I walked out of the restaurant, called a cab, and went back to the Martins'.

Mrs. Martin was reading in the den. The light was soft and warm, and there were peonies in the cloisonné vases. They were so full-blown, ready to scatter their pink petals at the slightest touch.

I told Mrs. Martin the whole story—well, most of it. Then I told her that I loved her like a mother but that I had to leave. She hugged me and kissed me and rubbed the lipstick stains off my cheek. There were tears in her eyes.

"I understand, Ruby," she said. "You're meant to have whatever your heart desires. Did you know that? Whatever your heart wants that much is already a part of you."

She didn't know that my desire was you and I couldn't tell her, but I know she really would have understood. Once she'd told me she grew up in a trailer park. On the wall above her bed was a magazine photo of a tall, blond woman with a broad smile and her two children, posing in a room among cloisonné vases filled with pink peonies.

Whatever your heart wants that much.

The next day I gave my notice and bought a plane ticket to England.

it might as well be me

THESE WERE THE THINGS I knew about you:

You were twenty-five years old. You were born in a small village in the English countryside, the only son of Isabelle and Phillip Woolf, a scholar, professor, and author of the acclaimed book *Fear of the Dark: The Repression of Magick in the Modern World*. Isabelle and Phillip still lived in the village, and Isabelle owned a small shop called Cauldron of Wisdom. You had performed in plays since you were a young child. At eighteen, you left home to study theater in London, where you were cast, almost immediately, as Hamlet and discovered by a talent scout from the States. After appearing in minor parts in a few films, you won the role of the angel disguised as a man, Lugh, in *Knights of the Sun*. This made you a star overnight. You were chosen as one of the most beautiful people in the world by one magazine and the most eligible bachelor of the year by another. Other interviews revealed that you were a daredevil, loved to travel, sky-dive, bungee-jump, horseback-ride, and sword-fight. You also read poetry and even wrote a bit. Keats was your favorite. You could recite *Endymion*. And Shakespeare's sonnets. Most of the money you made went to charitable causes for the environment and animals. You worshiped your mother and were looking for the perfect girl, but you knew she would come to you when the time was right, and meanwhile you were just enjoying your work, friends, and adventures. Some of this I found out on the Internet and at newsstands. Some of it I learned by sneaking into Mr. Martin's private office and looking up a file on you from the film he had produced. It was the only time I had done something dishonest to the Martins. I felt badly about it, but I also really didn't believe I had a choice not to do it.

I thought, someone has to get you, right? Look at all the wives of famous, brilliant, beautiful men. They had one thing in common, didn't they? At one point, they all said to themselves, it might as well be me. They did what had to be done.

There was one other thing about you. You had recently vanished from the public eye. No upcoming roles, no interviews, no recent photos in the tabloids. It was as if you had disappeared. Rumors were rampant that you were drugaddled, dying, or dead. Your publicist refused to comment in detail, only reassuring everyone that you were fine. There was nothing about this in Jack Martin's files.

Someone has to find you, I told myself.

It might as well be me.

IT WAS DAWN AND RAINING when I arrived in London. I took the underground to the hotel I'd found online. It was way over my budget, but I had decided I'd treat myself before I got serious about what I was doing here. The hotel was small and elegant, with a cozy, plush lobby. My suite smelled of lavender. There was a tiny, slightly sunken sitting room, botanical prints on the walls, soft, white towels wrapped in pale blue ribbons, and large windows that looked out over the fountains in the gardens beyond. The concierge had told me that Princess Di could be seen walking there when she was alive. I took a bubble bath and ordered a huge breakfast of poached eggs and pastries in my room. I was going to try to sleep for a while but I was too excited, so I went out right away and just started walking. My clogs clicked on the stone pavement and the rain netted my hair. I imagined being here with you. We would go to Hampstead Heath and the National Gallery and the Victoria and Albert and Buckingham Palace. We would go to Keats's house and read the original versions of his poetry, written in his hand, shielded behind glass and brocade. A poem about a shepherd so beautiful that the moon herself fell in love with him. I wanted to see everything, but not yet. I would see it with you. This I knew. Remember, Ruby, you have the knowing. Don't doubt it.

I stopped at a few shops and bought the clothes I had put on my list. A secondhand black riding jacket and pants, black riding boots, a white shirt, green cashmere sweater, a yellow silk skirt and blouse, a vintage green satin dress with a full skirt, high-heeled golden sandals and shiny red ones. I also got a large, emerald-green leather satchel that I couldn't resist. I had planned this carefully before I left (with only jeans, T-shirts, sneakers, a white cotton nightgown, and two handmade dresses packed into my suitcase along with my laptop, toiletries, and a few books), knowing about your love of horses, the color yellow, and your penchant for natural yet glamorous, adventurous yet nurturing, demure yet sexy women. That's what the silly fan magazines said, but I had decided not to discount anything.

The shopping took longer than I'd expected and made me hungry, so I went straight to dinner. I'd planned this as well. I knew you loved Indian food and you'd been spotted here more than once before. It was a tiny place, next to one of the iron-gated gardens that pop up every few blocks. The patio opened out onto the garden and there were lanterns hanging from the trees. I thought about my favorite childhood book, where the young heroine heals herself and her friend by taking him into the secret garden. Poor Mary—jaundiced and orphaned. I wondered what the contemporary version would be. Mary abused and cutting herself. Colin an up-and-coming star who has dropped out of the public eye to overcome his addictions. Maybe I'd write it. That was when it came to me—my new identity. I would tell anyone who asked that I was here to research and write a book. Someday that was what I would tell you.

You weren't at the restaurant. I saw a group of laughing boys with dark, curly hair and shiny eyes, but none of them were you. I ate channa masala and alu gobi and basmati rice, sopping up the sauce with the naan. Everything was warm, spicy, fragrant in the little metal dishes. Garlic, cardamom, cloves, ginger, fennel. My eyes watered so that I could hardly see. In the blur of my tears and the candlelight and the Indian beer I drank, one of the boys could almost have been you. But he wasn't.

For a moment, walking home, I felt afraid. The streets were deserted. I had assumed that in a city where the police are called bobbies, I wouldn't have much to worry about. But you never know. Even with a knowing. You can even be unsafe in your own home. You are unsafe everywhere when you've seen what I've seen. That's what I was thinking when I started to run.

I saw a pub and darted inside. It was dark and smoky, warm after the cool outside air. A group of people about my age were gathered around the bar. I bumped into a girl with a drink in her hand. She turned and grinned at me. She had long, curly, blond hair worn up in a bun and was dressed very chicly in a short tweed jacket, a silk blouse, jeans, high-heeled sandals, and strands of pearls and chains. I was startled when she kissed me on the cheek with her pretty mouth.

"Do I know you? Welcome to my party, even if I don't know you! What's your name?"

I told her and she started giggling. "Hello there, Ruby Tuesday. Come join the fun. I don't think I actually know you?"

She ordered me a drink and handed it to me. I gulped

it down all at once. A little while later, I was walking in a pack along the streets to the girl's flat. It was in a tall, white building overlooking a busy, brightly lit square. The rooms had polished wooden floors, filigreed white walls, and almost no furniture except for a large, green velvet chaise lounge in front of a fireplace. Someone put on some old funk music, and pretty soon everyone was dancing. I sat on cushions on the floor. The girl came over to me. She smelled of flowers, and I saw that there were tiny blossoms stuck in her hair now. She had put on more lipstick. Her mouth was very wide and her lips looked soft. She reached out and touched my arm.

The strangest sensation. I felt desire when she touched me. I pulled away and she smiled.

"It's all right. It's just a bit of a magic night. Everything you touch will make you feel like that."

What had she put in my drink? I watched as she danced away, rubbing her hands on the green velvet chaise as if it were alive.

I got a cab back to the hotel and packed my bags before I fell asleep.

It was time to leave London. Someday, I will come back here, I told myself. Not alone. I will see the Madonnas at the National Gallery and the dollhouses at the

Victoria and Albert. The changing of the guards. I will sip wine with you in a hidden, gated garden and make love with you in the starched, lavender-scented sheets of a hotel overlooking fountains and the home of a dead princess. This I knew.

HE WAS STANDING AT THE WINDOW *of his hotel suite, looking down at the pavement below. He was wondering how thick the glass was and if he kicked it, what would happen? Would it shatter? Would he fall?*

He didn't understand why he was thinking these thoughts. He had everything a young man could ask for. Here, in a room filled with champagne, chocolates, fresh sheets and towels, bouquets of yellow roses from his fans. There were girls waiting in the lobby, wearing yellow dresses and high heels, their hair back in ponytails, hoping to catch a glimpse of him. Some of them were crying into each other's perfumed necks. His new film was going to be released in a few days. Everyone was saying it would confirm his status as the most eligible bachelor and sexi-est man alive. Is that really what they were saying? He thought it was a load of shit, really. Who was it they were talking about? They liked his face and voice and his ab-dominal muscles. They admired how he could inhabit a character like some kind of shape-shifter. In a few years or months or days, they would choose someone else. His agent told him to enjoy it while it lasted, but he didn't know how to enjoy it at all.

He took another swig from the bottle of champagne and swished it around in his mouth. He was drinking too much. The back of his eye sockets ached with lack of sleep. His mother had told him to come home for a little while. She had heard something in his voice on the phone, even though he tried to disguise it.

She didn't ask too many questions, just said, "I'll bake you fresh scones every morning. You can roam the woods or sleep all day."

He saw the stretch limousines pulling into the circular drive. Their dark glass windows seemed foreboding, like eyes hiding emotional clues behind sunglasses. He saw the gray stone facade of the natural history museum across the street—a tomb for bones of extinct creatures. The glass-and-chrome shops filled with decapitated manne-quins now seemed ostentatious and even ominous instead of alluring. He felt the loneliness of fine hotel rooms, that cool, peaceful, haunting loneliness, the loneliness of clean sheets that countless other bodies have used before, and polished magnifying mirrors into which countless other faces have gazed, scrutinizing their imperfections.

He knew he would book a flight home tomorrow.

cauldron of wisdom

IT WAS LIKE SOMETHING out of one of those coffee table books, *The Most Picturesque Villages in England*. Meadows, fallow with autumn now, surrounded the little village with its curving, cobbled streets. The buildings were whitewashed with brown half-timbering or made of rich gray stone. Some leaned out as if begging me to touch them. The trees were huge, sprawling, overgrown with vines. I wanted to climb the trees so much, to hear their secrets. The wood smoke made me light-headed and the damp early-morning air clung to my skin like gossamer, but I felt grounded, my feet stepping solidly over the stones. I was at home, as if I'd been here before. The foliage and climate weren't so different from where I'd grown up. Maybe that was it. Or maybe I really had been in this place. There was some kind of enchantment. Even my memories that day were only the sweet ones, as if the demons were not allowed here.

IN THE AUTUMN, my whole family would walk to the high school to watch the evening football games. We'd crunch through the backyards full of red, brown, and golden leaves. The air smelled like bonfires, and later my hair would be a cloud of wood smoke. We'd sit on the bleachers and watch the game and eat hot dogs and drink root beer. My father was happy then. The whole town knew him. People used to joke that he was so popular he could have been mayor. It always amazed me and Opal how well he could deceive them. There were times we wanted to believe in this fantasy father, too.

When we got home at night, Opal and I couldn't always fall asleep right away. It was cold, and we'd meet in the hallway, squatting over the floor heater in our thin nightgowns, letting the warm air blow up onto our legs. We didn't say much, just sat there together.

On Halloween, my mother always helped us make our costumes. We were usually black cats. We sewed headbands with ears and made fuzzy tails for our one-piece body suits. Every year, Mom was a witch in a huge pointy hat and green face paint. She put dry ice in a big cauldron and stood on our front porch, cackling. She had sharp incisors—I got them from her—and when she laughed, you could see them. It used to terrify me when I was little. I'd have dreams about her trying to bite me with those teeth. But on Halloween, it was fun. We gave out candy corn that made our molars ache and then we ate grilled cheese sandwiches and drank milkshakes while the lights flickered out in the jack-o'-lanterns.

One Halloween, Tommy Walden and I dressed up as ghouls. It felt good to become the monsters instead of always fighting them off. Tommy was small and scrappy, with a forelock of hair that fell into his eyes. He and I ran through the fields screaming at the top of our lungs, collapsing in the tall grasses. We climbed trees and sat up there all day practicing bird calls. We'd dare each other to jump out in front of cars on the road, then run off and dive into the bushes, breathless and laughing, when the driver hit the brakes. We did that on Halloween, too, immortal in our black clothes and fluorescent face paint. No cars would possibly hit us. He was my best friend, and I was so sad when we had to move away again. Later, I found out his mom had a new baby and he insisted she name her after me.

So it wasn't all bad, where I came from. It wasn't all bad.

I HAD DONE MY RESEARCH on the village, so I recognized the pub right away. It was a pale yellow building, intricately half-timbered. But I hadn't seen a picture of the inside. The walls were paneled with large rectangles of dark wood. There were a few small, square wooden tables, scrubbed clean, with candles dripping their wax into strange sculptures. Other candles burned in sconces on the walls. Toward the back of the room was a dark, shiny wooden bar and some red-leather bar stools. A large stuffed raven was perched on a stick above a print of a winter wheat field where a crow in old-fashioned lace-up boots posed under a gray sky. There were other pictures on the walls, too. Silvery, distorted tintypes, black-and-white shots from the fifties and more recent pictures of family patrons, local war heroes, cricket teams, May fair queens. None of the pictures made me take a second glance. Until I saw the autographed head shot. But even that was not what made my heart stop pumping blood; I had seen pictures of you like this before. It was the picture of the scrappy little boy with a fishing rod and bucket. Maybe he reminded me of Tommy Walden because I had just been thinking about him, but that is what I thought of—splashing through the river in big rubber boots with Tommy Walden. Maybe because of Tommy Walden I felt I already knew that little boy grinning under his cotton fisherman's hat. Maybe I felt I knew him already because he was you.

I had worked as a bartender back home for a while. It was at this little place at the edge of town, with sawdust on the floors and TVs blaring all day and night. The owners, May and Rupe Cling, were kind to me. They said I was like their own daughter. But once Artis Woodbridge's nephew Darryl came in there. He said that he remembered me from school and he'd heard I'd moved here, too. He was a tall, handsome, athletic-looking guy studying law at the local university. So nice. I told him I'd love to have a drink with him after work. But the attitude the Clings gave him in the bar! It was disgusting. Darryl spent most of the evening talking about how weirdly they treated him and what a messed-up town and he couldn't wait to get the hell out of there. I agreed with him and tried to make him feel better but I knew it was too late. He called me once after that and said, "Ruby, you are a lovely young lady and I enjoyed your company but I just can't handle the vibes." And that was that. I knew it wasn't that unusual and that it could happen almost anywhere, but I also knew that nothing like that would happen here. White, black, and Pakistani people were drinking together. The mingling voices had a lulling sound. A short, plump, round-faced woman was scurrying around, clucking, making sure everyone had what they needed. She came over to me with a big smile.

"You're new in town? Nice to have visitors. Can I get you something? We brew our own ale."

I told her I'd love some and we got to talking. Her name was Marge Bentley and she and her husband, Edward, owned the pub and the nearby inn. I told her I'd read up on their establishments, and she was delighted about that. She kept refilling my glass and showed me all around, introducing me to everyone, and by evening I felt as if she were some kind of long-lost auntie.

Edward, her mild-mannered, towering spouse, got me a room at the inn, and that night, when I slid into the small, dark bed with the bright white sheets, in a room smelling of cedar, I slept better than I had in years and maybe a lifetime.

The Bentleys' inn resembled an overgrown dollhouse. I kept wanting to be able to see what it looked like without the back wall, to peer into tiny, wallpapered rooms with everything set neatly in its place—the needlepoint settee, the velvet love seats and tasseled cushions and handmade lace curtains.

It stood on the edge of a lake. In the gray dawn, the ducks and swans glided through the fog like fragments of someone's dreams. The willow trees swung their hair into the water. I walked around and around until I was sweating. Then I went inside and drank tea and ate fruit and the home-baked blackberry scones the size of small loaves of bread, which Marge had set out on the dining-room sideboard. I was the only guest.

It was the time of year, Marge said. Not many tourists. She was interested in the book I was writing. She showed me photos of the house dating back to the turn of the century and told me about the yellow daffodils that grew in the spring, the spa—a natural hot spring with healing powers—the ancient ground sculpture of the phallic man that could only be seen from the air. I wanted so much to ask her about the young actor who grew up in this village and then vanished from the public eye. I could almost have gotten away with it, because of your picture in the pub, but I had to bite my lip until I felt the marks of my teeth. When she was done, I thanked her and went into town.

I wanted to skip, but I restrained myself. Don't draw attention, nothing flashy or strange, Ruby. Although somehow I felt that no one would really mind here. There was an undercurrent of eccentricity in the village. One house had antique china doll heads filling the casement window. Most of them were bald and a few had only one eye. There was a bakery with breads in the shapes of small, round, bare-breasted women on display. The smell of warm dough made me hungry. A bent old woman passed me, pushing a cart filled with daisies and wearing a giant hat that looked as if it had been made from bare winter branches swathed in tulle. She was followed by a trail of cats, two of whom wore decorated hats of their own. I kept walking until I saw what I had been looking for—a gray stone building with rose vines climbing up the walls. I stopped and took a breath. Above hung a wooden sign in the shape of a pig: CAULDRON OF WISDOM. I crossed the street and walked right up to the door. There was another sign: ALL SEEK-ERS OF CERRIDWEN ENTER AND FIND PEACE.

I went in slowly, not wanting to make a sound, but the heavy wooden door bumped into a cluster of bells suspended from the low ceiling just above the door. It was dark inside, with a few rays of autumn light filtering in through an open leaded-glass window. There were three doorways, each leading to small rooms filled with some of the oddest things I had ever seen.

One room was like a kitchen, with a wooden floor and a black iron wood-burning stove. Twig brooms covered one wall. From the ceiling hung bundles of sage and dried herbs. I could recognize rosemary and lavender, and there were other scents, too—strange and earthy. Small wooden tables displayed bowls of carved wood and stone, baskets of leaves, feathers, pinecones, and shells; black, white, green, purple, and red candles; and incense sticks and burners. Also some funny-looking dolls with soft, wrinkled faces, which I realized were made from dried apples with raisin eyes and grains of rice stuck into them for teeth. Stones and rocks of various shapes and sizes were stacked loosely or arranged in formations. The room had a door that led into a tiny glass greenhouse filled with exotic-looking plants.

The next room was like a study, with cases of leather-bound books on every wall. A fire burned behind an iron grate, and large tapestry cushions were arranged in front of it. All around were tall, obelisk-shaped glass cases full of altar tools. There were knives, daggers, chalices, and the wooden or metal athames for circle casting. Other cases displayed tarot cards and runes. One smaller case contained small blue bottles of liquid. Someone had handwritten the labels in a cramped, spidery script that I couldn't quite make out.

The third room smelled sweet from the vases of hothouse roses. The scent and the velvet chaise longues piled with silk pillows made me want to lie down here. There were framed moon charts on the walls. Some were ancient, ready to disintegrate behind the glass. Silk-velvet hooded cloaks in shimmery, pale colors hung on a rack. In the middle of the room was a round glass case lined with dark blue and purple velvet and filled with crystals, white chalcedonies, aquamarines, opals, bloodstones, rubies, and moonstones. I could also see tiny velvet drawstring pouches with mirrors peeking out from inside of them.

I was looking at the case when I heard someone coming from another room at the back of the store.

"Oh, I didn't hear the door! Welcome."

She was a slender woman in her late forties, with dark hair that had started to go silver. Her eyes were large and dark, with thick eyelashes, and she had a small space between her lips, even when they were closed. I recognized that mouth. It had been analyzed and praised in the magazine that chose you as one of the most beautiful people in the world. I stood there gazing at her, trying to understand how this could have come to pass.

How I could be talking to your mother.

"Thank you," I said.

"You're American?"

"I'm afraid so."

"No, it's lovely. We don't get too many visitors from the States here. I'd better make a nice impression and offer you some tea."

"I'd love that."

I followed her into the kitchen, where she boiled water on the stove. I wanted to just stare and stare. She had a long, slender neck. A few tendrils of hair had escaped her bun. She had given birth to you; this body had contained you and brought you out into the world.

"Are you on holiday?" she asked.

"Actually I'm living here for a while. I'm staying at the Bentleys'."

"Whatever made you come to our lazy little village?"

She was looking at me with her warm eyes and I felt shy all of a sudden. "I'm a writer, well, sort of, and I thought living in the English countryside would be kind of inspiring."

"My husband will be delighted. He's a writer himself. Phillip Woolf. And I'm Isabelle."

"I'm Ruby. Pleased to meet you."

"And you, dear." She asked if I'd seen the rubies in the case.

"Yes, they're beautiful."

"And you're familiar with the lore?"

I nodded.

"Well it's always good to have a ruby around," Isabelle said.

Your mother, Isabelle.

All of a sudden, I wanted to leave. It was going too well, too easily. I was afraid something would happen to spoil it.

"I have to go," I said. "But thank you so much for everything."

"What about your tea?" she asked me.

I apologized and thanked her and told her I would be back. It was too much for me at that moment.

Before I left, she pressed something into my hand.

"A gift," she said.

It was one of the small blue bottles with liquid inside. I could read the label. The label said CRONE-WISDOM.

the crone

THIS IS WHAT I REMEMBER for certain:

I left the village and went into the meadow. I walked over the sparse grasses to a stile, crossed that, went down a winding road, and came to the forest. The trees grew close together. They were turning gold with autumn. The sun had come out and it filled the leaves so that they shimmered, almost metallic. The sound of the birds and the shining leaves seemed to blend together, to be almost one thing. I opened the blue bottle and swallowed all the contents in one gulp. Then I walked into the woods. This is what I remember. This is what happened. But there was more. The rest felt even more real. Did it happen, too?

. . .

I AM IN A DARK FOREST on a narrow, winding path. I feel lost, like a child in a fairy tale, a panic pressing on my chest, but I take a deep breath to dissolve it and keep walking. The trees are ancient—oak, pines, elders. They are shivering without their foliage, stripped bare with winter. I shiver, too, wondering why I didn't dress more warmly. I hear birds, but not musical chirping—a haunting sound that echoes in the trees. I sense the presence of large, fierce animals lurking, but I don't see any. The path curves through to a clearing. At the far end is a cob cottage with a thatched roof. On each side of the door is a row of sturdy-looking flowers with pearly, white, large, almost orchid-shaped blossoms that seem to gleam with an inner light. I go closer, squinting to see better. They aren't flowers at all but skulls, human skulls on thin stakes, bleached white from being dried in the sun.

Now the panic in my chest is a creature squatting there, but before I can turn away, an old woman appears in the doorway. She's like a part of the forest in her earth-brown robes. Her hair seems to be changing back and forth from thin and white to thick, shiny, and black, and her eyes change, too. First pale and clouded with cataracts, then black and sparkling.

Now her hair stays white and her eyes dark. She motions for me to walk to her, and I feel my feet moving forward. The wrong way—I need to leave. I stop in front of her, so close I can feel her icy breath. There is a moment of complete stillness. Then she snatches my hand—a cat pouncing on its prey. Her own hands are bony and leathery. She strokes my palm. I am freezing. I am hollow. Cavernous.

She turns my palm facedown and gently strokes the top of my hand. Now I am warm, heat radiating out of me. I am the sun.

"What do you want, my child, that is not already a part of you?"

I hear my voice as if it belongs to someone else. Someone young and afraid, crouched on the floor of a bathroom in the Midwest behind a rattling door. A child who can ask for nothing, not even the protection of a lock. "What am I allowed to want?"

"Allowed?" she howls. "Allowed?" Her voice is a wind in my chest. "You are allowed to seek anything that is already a part of you."

But what is a part of me? The sun god? The goddess? The demon?

I REMEMBER LYING on the end-of-spring grass, the most lush and tender. A breeze lifting the tips of my hair very gently, the sun shining down. Earth, wind, fire. How well they work together. The sun is so warm and comforting it almost tickles.

Later, I told my mother about lying in the sunshine. She looked at me closely.

"Ruby, the sun kissed you!"

"How do you know that?"

"Well come look in the mirror. There are little sun kisses all over your nose and cheeks."

So we went to the mirror together. I leaned in so close that my nose was nearly touching the glass, my breath making funny marks. And there they were—the reddish-brown spots sprinkled over my cheeks, below my eyes and over the bridge of my nose. I touched one gently, not wanting to rub it off.

My mother whispered in my ear: "The sun must think you are something special, Ruby. He doesn't kiss just anyone and he kissed you, see, very delicately." She pointed to a tiny speck on my nose.

I leaned in again, looking at the sun's gifts. When I closed my eyes, I could feel him again.

YOU KISSED ME all those years ago, but if I find you, will you remember?

. . .

I RAN BACK to Isabelle's shop the next day.

"And how are you this morning, Miss Ruby?"

"What was in that potion you gave me?" I asked.

"Oh, just some herbs and flower essences. Black walnut— I thought it might help you with your writing project."

I leaned against the wall and tried to catch my breath.

"What's wrong, dear?"

She led me to the back of the store. There was a wooden door marked NO ADMITTANCE, which she unlocked with a key on a cord around her neck. The first thing I noticed was a large, black, beveled mirror propped up on a low table, surrounded by colored candles of various shapes and sizes. The smell of beeswax was so strong I thought I could taste honey on my lips. There was another table, with a black cauldron, a wooden mortar and pestle, and small bowls full of powders. A bookcase held some very ancient-looking leather-bound volumes. In one corner was an altar, draped in purple velvet and covered with crystals, gemstones, roses, and small picture frames with their backs facing outward so I could not see the photos in them.

Isabelle sat me down at the table with the mirror and put her delicate hand over mine.

"Now, tell me."

I shook my head. "I just swallowed the potion and I felt a little funny afterwards."

"I'm so sorry, Ruby. I should have told you, it's on the label but I should have said, you just rushed off so quickly. It's all completely harmless ingredients but I suggest you only take ten drops at a time in a little warm spring water. I feel just terrible."

I reassured her that I was fine. She watched me for a while. Then she said, "You have a bit of the gift, don't you?"

I knew she meant the knowing, but I felt uncomfortable about it, so I looked down.

"Do you mind if I give you a reading? Nothing fancy, just a quick tarot. It would be on the house. To make up for my negligence with the crone, if that would be all right?"

Suddenly, I was afraid again. What would she see in my cards? That I loved her son? That my father beat me? That I was completely and utterly insane? Something even worse?

But I let her do it. Everything was going so smoothly, and I knew she had a sense about me; that seemed like a good sign.

Isabelle shuffled the cards and carefully laid them out

in a formation. She studied them without saying anything. I could see that she was trying not to show much expression.

I didn't know a lot about tarot, but some of the cards weren't hard to figure out. The first card showed two dogs looking up at a yellow moon in a blue sky. There was also a lobster crawling out of the water, and two odd towers. I had always liked moon imagery, but for some reason the card made me feel uneasy. Isabelle put a card horizontally over "The Moon," crossing it. This card showed a bare-chested, bearded, horned creature with goat legs, chicken feet, and a pentacle on its forehead crouched above a naked, horned couple who were bound together with a chain. "The Devil." I knew who that was. Above the first two cards was a woman seated on an ornate throne, holding a large golden vessel. I liked that one. "The Queen of Cups." And I liked "The High Priestess," a woman in a pale blue robe sitting on a throne between two columns with pomegranates behind her. The next card was "The Tower." Two men were falling out of a burning building. Isabelle tapped her finger on it, a little nervously, I thought. She saw me eyeing the "Death" card with a skeleton in armor riding a white horse.

"Don't worry," she said. Her smile seemed slightly

forced though. "Death is transformation. It's actually quite positive."

Somehow I wasn't fully buying that. I watched her put down a few more cards. A graceful woman with a bird perched on her hand standing among vines of red grapes and nine golden pentacles. A man lying on his stomach with ten swords piercing his spine. This time I was sure I saw Isabelle flinch, but she kept going. A man with his arm around a woman stood beside two dancing children under a rainbow of golden cups. The last card she laid out showed a naked, fair-haired child with a crown of flowers, riding on a white pony in front of a wall of sunflowers. A large yellow sun shone in the sky above.

Isabelle smiled up at me. "I knew you were meant to come," she said. "Are you free for dinner tonight, Ruby?"

What had she seen? It didn't matter. I was one step closer to the sun.

fear of the dark

I WENT TO THE HOUSE that night. It was a stone cottage with a dark, thatched roof—the kind I would have thought didn't exist anymore if I hadn't researched the village already—and a small garden. Pumpkins grew on vines in the front beds, beside the Michaelmas daisies. There was a stone well that made the place seem even more like a fairy-tale illustration.

As I walked up to the door, a woman with skin so dark and smooth it seemed painted on came out of the house and brushed past. Our eyes met, and I had the feeling she was seeing some kind of X-ray image of me. I greeted her but she didn't say a word.

Inside, the house was much different from Isabelle's

shop. There was none of the clutter or mystery. Everything was bright and fresh.

I helped Isabelle set the wooden table in front of the kitchen fireplace. There was home-baked bread, a wheel of cheese, and a pot of rich vegetable stew for dinner. Isabelle apologized for the simple meal.

"It's my favorite," I told her. "My mother used to tell me I'd turn into a mouse or a rabbit."

A man walked in and took off his hat to me. I knew right away he was your father. He was tall and wiry, with twinkling eyes and a firm, dry handshake.

"Phillip Woolf. You must be Ruby."

I nodded. "Pleased to meet you, sir."

"Sir? Please. Phillip."

He offered me a glass of red wine and we sat in small velvet armchairs in the front room while the stew finished cooking.

"Isabelle told me you're new here."

"Yes, I just arrived. It's so lovely."

"My wife likes to make everyone feel at home but she has a special feeling about you, I think."

"I'm honored," I said. I didn't want to talk about myself, though. I was afraid he might find something out. "Isabelle says you're a writer? Your book sounds fascinating."

"I hope so. It tends to be a bit dry, I'm told. But the subject might interest you. The sacred feminine is gathering so much force, even in popular culture. But the male energy can't quite handle it. It's all somewhat explosive."

"Do you think that's why there's so much turmoil now?"

"Until there is more acceptance of the feminine, it'll be a struggle. It's too threatening. But some people want change."

"Not where I come from." After I'd said it, I wished I hadn't. I didn't want him to know I had even a hint of bitterness about my past.

"We're sheltered here. Everyone in this village seems to be of the same mind."

"How wonderful. You must never want to leave!"

He smiled and took Isabelle's hand. "I must say there isn't much I could want in the world. But when you're young it's a different story, isn't it?"

He looked melancholy for a moment, and I wondered if he was thinking of you.

Where were you? All of a sudden, the question started up in me, almost a panic. Don't panic, Ruby. You've come this far. And it's been so easy. Like a miracle. You're in the Woolfs' house! You're here. Just don't blow it. Don't ask.

After dinner, we sat in soft armchairs by the fireplace and ate apple crisp. The thin sheets of brown sugar crumbled in my mouth. I felt warm and cozy, so relaxed that it scared me. I didn't want to slip.

I asked Phillip more about his work.

"She's the inspiration." When he looked over at his wife, his eyes shone like little fireplaces and I wondered if I'd ever be that infatuated with someone after so many years.

I thought about the title of Phillip's book. Fear of the dark. I prided myself on my appreciation of the goddess, the moon, secrets of the night. But I was afraid of the darkness, too. Suddenly I wanted to tell this to Phillip, have him look at me the way a concerned father would. *People who are afraid of the dark, if they understand the natural feminine forces, they must have seen something, something unnatural.* I could almost hear him saying the words.

Fear of the dark. Witches with boils on their faces under the bed. Goblins expelling sulfuric gas in the closet. A circle of men around me, the same pale, small-featured male mask on all their faces. My father's face. At bedtime, I turned off the overhead light switch at the door and jumped all the way across to my mattress so my feet wouldn't touch the floor.

I took a sip of tea, scalded my tongue, and winced. The pain in my mouth felt almost good, though, a warning for me not to say too much.

So I didn't tell Phillip or Isabelle about my fear of the dark. Or why I had that fear at all.

This is all that Phillip and Isabelle knew about me when I left that night:

I was from the Midwest. We had always lived in the same home—a bright white structure with green shutters and a wraparound porch overlooking marshlands. We had a greenhouse where my mother grew the exotic flowers she sold at her florist shop. My father was a veterinarian and taught at the college. We always had lots of animals that were like part of the family. I spent my days roaming the woods and fields, looking for injured birds to save. I used a dropper to feed them worms ground up in a blender mixed with Gatorade. My parents were very relaxed and lenient, except that they protected my sister, Opal, and me from popular culture, so we were a bit naive. We knew all the classic novels but none of the current movies. I told Phillip and Isabelle the memories that came back when I got to their village—the smell of bonfires, crunching through the leaves on the way to the football games, root beer and hotdogs, grilled cheese and milkshakes, Halloween and Tommy Walden.

Because I was so at home and because they were so attentive, it didn't feel as if I were lying. I began to feel that all of it was real.

spells of invisibility

I ENDED UP WORKING at Isabelle's shop. It was just another miracle in a series of miracles that were leading me to you, and I didn't question it. When she asked, I just thanked her and told her I'd be there in the morning.

The days passed and I almost stopped thinking about you. Not because I had given up hope. I was just so happy. I was the happiest I had ever been. In the morning, I walked around the lake, had tea and scones with Marge Bentley, and went to the shop. I spent the day sorting and pricing new merchandise or selling candles and crystals and potions to the men and women of the village. It was amazing to me how many of these folk used magic. It was just part of their lives, like afternoon tea or buying the paper. People of every age and race came in there. There were a few you'd expect, like the teenagers with punky hair and earth mothers in their paisley dresses, but businessmen and waitresses, plumbers and librarians came, too. I loved helping them; they all seemed so delighted with their purchases as if they were carrying home little bits of love and prosperity in their bags.

Isabelle and I ate lunch together when there was a lull. Fellow rabbit-mice that we were, we usually had cheese sandwiches on dark bread and some raw vegetables and fruit. In the evenings, she invited me to dinner sometimes. Other nights I spent alone wandering around the village, eating at one of the local restaurants or sitting at the pub. People started to know my name and I felt very at home, but I didn't get too close to anyone. It was safer that way and I liked having a little aura of mystery. On my days off I went riding in the countryside or walked through the woods. That was my favorite thing to do. Nothing strange happened after the first time I'd seen the crone but there was still that sensation of possibility, as if the trees might start talking to me or the fairy lights of my childhood appear in the shallow creek that ran through the forest.

And I wanted magic. All of it. I wanted to be able to go into the darkest darkness without fear.

That was when Isabelle gave me her book of shadows. She was smiling, and her voice had a light tone even
though the book felt so dark and heavy in my hands, so
full of secrets.

"Just give it a go. See what interests you. Have fun."

Of course I chose what I chose. It felt like the most
important thing. I could have chosen a love spell but I
wasn't ready yet. I didn't have the strength and I wasn't
whole enough. I was still too afraid of the dark.

THE MOON was waning.

Every night I took a bath with sandalwood oil. Then
I lit a black candle anointed with the same oil. I took off
my robe, lay down on the bed on my side, curled up into
a fetal position, and closed my eyes. As I tried to deepen
and regulate my breathing, I imagined the dimensions of
the bed. I saw the comforter, each petal of each cabbage
rose, each vein of each leaf. The colors made me feel different ways. The reds and pinks made me warmer, the
greens made me cooler, the white background made me
feel as if I were floating away. The bed was firm, and my
body absorbed the subtle vibrations of the mattress. It
began to take on the energy of the bed, the texture and
density and shape. I imagined the whole bed enveloping
and shielding me.

On the night when the moon was black, I performed the ritual wearing a long, silvery-blue silk-velvet robe that Isabelle had made for me, and then I walked out of the Bentleys' and went to the pub. I sat there all night but no one took my order or spoke to me. I was going to go into the woods and dance in the darkness, fearless, but I realized that I didn't want to be invisible anymore. I didn't have to hide here. I wanted to be as visible as possible. I wanted you to recognize me.

I wish I had known how to become invisible at times when I was a child, though. I could have used it then.

SOMETIMES MY FATHER went away on business or on a hunting or fishing trip. My mother and Opal and I felt so free. We stayed up late, having marshmallows and popcorn for dinner, and watching TV. We made fun of the commercials and created our own lines to the jingles, laughing so hard our ribs ached and tears poured down our faces.

On those nights I didn't need to be invisible. I didn't need a night-light. I wasn't afraid of the dark.

the wish

WHEN I WAS A LITTLE GIRL, I went to a magic show with
my family. The magician was a tall man with the face of
a 1920s matinee idol and hands like birds. I sat there,
trying not to breathe, so I could catch every movement
he made. I kept thinking, how could we all be sitting
here so calmly while he is demonstrating such mystical
powers?

He produced a huge bunch of long-stemmed red
roses.

"They're magic," he said. "I will give one to a member
of the audience who holds the power to manifest dreams
as reality."

He walked away from the stage lights so he would

be able to see all of our faces. I sat completely motionless, knowing he was going to give that rose to me. As he approached the row I was seated in, our eyes met and neither of us looked away. He walked straight to me and held out the rose. I still remember how cool the petals felt and the way it smelled. Like hope.

"This is for you, sweetheart. Put it under your pillow tonight and your dreams will come true."

He backed slightly away, turned, and went to the stage.

My father was sitting next to me, tapping his cigarette pack on his kneecap, but he didn't say anything. It was another time that we both knew I had won.

THERE HAD BEEN A LOT of blessings in my life. I did not have to doubt. That's what I kept telling myself.

AND THEN ISABELLE INVITED me over for dinner again. She said she needed to speak with me about something.

I sat nervously at the table, my leg bouncing noiselessly, hidden by the linen cloth. Isabelle had excused herself after we cleared away the dishes, and Phillip was busy in the kitchen, making us tea. He returned with a silver tray and Isabelle came after him. I noticed she seemed nervous, too, unlike her usually calm self.

Phillip served the tea and then sat down beside Isabelle across the table from me.

"Ruby, Phillip and I have a favor to ask you. It's a bit of an imposition so we'll understand if you decline."

A favor, I thought, thank God. They haven't discovered why I'm here.

"Of course. You know I'd do anything for you. You've both been so kind to me. Just name it."

"Oh, you're such a love, but hear us out first before you agree."

"Yes, Ruby, you must hear the terms first, we insist."

"Okay, whatever you want." The nervousness was creeping back up my neck.

Isabelle said, "We need to go away for the Christmas holiday. I'll be closing the shop so you won't have your responsibilities there." She paused. "We would like you to house-sit for us."

I sat forward to respond, but Phillip held up his hand and shook his head slightly. "That's not all. It's far more complicated."

They glanced at each other and Isabelle continued. "Yes, well, Ruby, you see we need you to take care of someone for us."

She couldn't mean what I was thinking. Not you. No, she must mean a cat or a dog, not you. My mind was racing and my heart was pounding so loudly I was sure they could hear it.

"It's our son, Orion. You may have heard of him."

I could hear her speaking but far away. The blood in my veins was all rushing to my head. Get a grip, Ruby. Get a grip.

". . . Well the fall was horrible. It's a wonder he survived at all. He keeps telling us something spooked the horse . . ."

She wasn't making sense. I looked at Phillip.

"Anyway, he's recovering here at home, in private. It is very important to him and to us that no one finds out. He feels it would be detrimental to his career and we want him to recover in peace and quiet." He paused, searching my face. I tried not to show too much emotion. "There is some care involved but mostly we just need you to be here. He has a nurse that comes once a day and a physical therapist as well."

"He's very depressed and fragile." Tears welled up in Isabelle's eyes, making them look even darker. "He will barely speak to anyone but we keep talking to him every day and sometimes I read to him." She covered her face with her hands and Phillip put his arms around her.

"We trust you completely. We know we are asking a

lot but quite frankly we need some time away." Phillip's strong voice wavered slightly for the first time.

My mouth was too dry; I didn't know how I was going to answer. I saw them sitting there, Isabelle still covering her face and Phillip looking so tired. Why hadn't I noticed how sad and tired they looked before? Were they covering it up or was I just too caught up in my fantasy to have seen?

"Of course I'll do it."

Isabelle's head snapped up. She was really letting herself cry now. "Oh, my lovely Ruby. I knew we could count on you. You've never even asked if he was our son. Most people ask me straight away."

"You are like a miracle. The way you just showed up in our lives." Phillip reached across the table and held my hand.

I looked down so he couldn't see the shame in my eyes. He stood up.

"All right, ladies, enough sadness. This is a happy moment. If Isabelle has taught me anything she's taught me that there are no coincidences."

"Let me take you home," Isabelle said, "so you can think about all we've dumped in your lap. You can come over again tomorrow and we'll show you everything and introduce you to Marie-Therese. And, of course, Orion."

My stomach lurched at the sound of your name. I stood up, but my legs were so weak that I had to steady myself on the table.

When she dropped me off, Isabelle hugged me and whispered in my ear, "You are such a gem. Your mother couldn't have chosen a better name."

I sat up, awake, most of the night. Too excited, too stunned to sleep. My mind kept playing the evening over and over.

You're here. You've been here all along.

I WALKED INTO THE ROOM. The curtains were pulled close to keep out the light. All I saw was a bed and a figure lying there.

"Ruby, come here, sweetness," Isabelle said. "I want you to meet my son."

I walked closer. You were lying in traction, strapped to an elaborate hospital bed that could be moved in various ways. You had lost a lot of weight, so every sinew of your body was defined. The cut of your cheekbones looked severe, stark. Your eyes were more haunting than ever. They seemed to be moving deeper into their sockets even as I watched.

I looked into your face. "Hello, Orion."

All my joy at being with you was not what I had expected. Because there was this other thing, this sorrow. You lay there broken, and if you had not been broken, my dream would not have come true. I would never have been there with you if you had not been hurt. What had I wished for? What had I created?

miss flora and the demon

IT SHOULD HAVE BEEN EASY for me to keep pretending and repressing. After all, I had spent my whole childhood doing these things. But when Isabelle and Phillip left, I started wondering if the whole idea was a big mistake.

Partly, it was because of Christmas. I had only been away from my family once before at this time of year, with the Martins, and part of me wished I could be home, baking sugar-crusted chocolate bourbon balls and Christmas cookies in the shapes of stars, bells, and angels with my mom and Opal. I tried to imagine sitting at my mother's table with you beside me, your back healed, your voice merry as you drank hot cider and chatted away with them. But even with my imagination, I couldn't see it. My old life was fading and you were lying in your bed, silent and sullen, hardly eating, avoiding my eyes now when I came to check on you. Fading, too.

That was the other reason I thought I'd made a mistake. You seemed so depressed and nothing I did was helping. What did I expect? Magic? Who did I think I was?

Before Isabelle left, she decorated the house with evergreen boughs, holly wreaths, mistletoe, bowls of nuts and fruits, candles, gold and silver moons and stars. Every nook and cranny was draped in folds of rich dark green velvet. It did look magical, and I began to think maybe I should at least try to do some spells of my own. Maybe I could cheer you up a little at least. So I spent the whole day on the meal. There was a rich mushroom risotto, crusty bread, a tray of cheeses, mulled wine, sweet spiced nuts, a glazed poppy-seed loaf, and the cookies I had imagined making with my mother.

I draped a green velvet cloth over my arm and balanced two large trays on either hand. Those years of waitressing as a teenager had paid off a little. You looked up.

"May I come in?"

You nodded. Your eyes widened a little at the food, but you didn't say a word.

I set the trays down and lit the candles I had placed all around your room. Outside, the garden was white under a black sky.

"This is only the second time I've been away from my family during the holidays. I thought I'd share some of our traditions with you."

I fed you small bites of all the dishes, but I kept my eyes averted, the way I always did when I helped you eat. I sensed the shame you felt at having to be cared for this way. I wanted to tell you that it was okay, that there was no reason to be ashamed with me, but I didn't want to make it worse.

When we were done eating, I said, "My mom used to read us this one book every Christmas Eve and I wanted to read it to you."

You didn't say anything, so I picked up *Miss Flora McFlimsey's Christmas Eve*. I kept it in a plastic envelope to protect the fragile cover—a pastel watercolor of a doll in a rocking chair—from completely disintegrating, like dried roses. The pale lavender and pink had rubbed off, so it looked as if white rose petals or drifts of snow were falling around Flora.

I read to you about the old doll locked in the attic, her only friend a mouse named Timothy. One night, the mouse tells the lonely doll that "there are strange goings-on downstairs." She realizes that it must be Christmas Eve and longs to have one look at the Christmas tree. Then, by sheer determination or perhaps magic, she can walk.

Out of the corner of my eye, I saw you flinch and I almost stopped reading. But somehow it seemed as if I should go on, even if it made you uncomfortable. It struck me as odd and somehow prophetic that this was the only book I had brought from home when I came here.

The doll goes carefully down the stairs and finds a frantic Santa Claus who has just discovered he is one doll short. Seeing Flora peeking out from behind a chair, he decides to use her as a replacement.

Sitting under the Christmas tree, she is filled with pride until she hears two brand-new dolls whispering unkind things about her. She tries to go back to the attic but finds once again her legs are frozen, and she begins to cry real tears.

I heard your breathing deepen from where you lay in the shadows. The candles were low now, wax pooling in the saucers, a thick scent of honey filling the room as the light was about to go out altogether.

"'What happened next could never be explained.'"

The angel from the top of the Christmas tree comes

down and helps Flora into her long-lost blue velvet dress and hat and her ermine muff so that she looks just as she had on that first Christmas long ago.

"'Then she leaned down and kissed Flora McFlimsey on her round rosy cheek and whispered something ever so softly in her ear. It was something about love, but only Miss Flora McFlimsey heard her.'"

In the morning, the children discover Flora, giving her all the love she has dreamed about for so long.

I closed the book quietly. I couldn't look at you. I stood up to leave.

Your voice sounded strange and I realized that your teeth must be clenched. "Is that it? Am I supposed to believe in miracles now? Was that children's story supposed to somehow give me a pathetic shred of hope? Where is my angel, Ruby? Is it you? Or do you see yourself as the little mouse?"

I turned to look at you, ready to answer with the same sarcasm until I saw your face. It was wet with your tears.

So I went back downstairs without saying a word. You were right.

Who do you think you are, Ruby? His friend? His savior?

The Christmas tree resembled the one in the book,

diffused by the glow of its own lights like a watercolor painting. I wanted to tell you that Flora McFlimsey was me, not you. Wishing for an angel. All I had were demons.

WE CALL IT the pit.

It is actually a pond in the middle of an old rock quarry. Sometimes I wish I could stay there for an entire year and watch the changes. Autumn: the air smells of smoke and the leaves dress the water in gowns of red, orange, and gold. In winter, the trees are black against the white snow, the world a silhouette as we skate over the ice. By springtime, everything is budding and blooming, the ground squelchy with rain. We sit on the rocks and drink beer, smoke joints, wait for the water to get warmer, because in the summer humidity, we will take off our clothes and plunge into the blue.

And now it is summer. The air is hot and heavy like in midafternoon, even though it is the darkest part of night. The water is as slick and dark as a black lacquered tabletop and the sky is just as dark, because the moon is gone.

You take off your shirt and then your jeans and shorts. I watch you dive off a rock into the water and disappear. Your head pops up.

"Come on!"

I remove my dress, aware of the fact that I am naked beneath it and that you are watching me. When the water touches me, I gasp at the cold against the heat of my skin.

"It's better if you get everything wet!" you shout. You are just a glow in the darkness.

My body is prickling with goose bumps and I can hear my teeth clattering together.

I tread water and turn in circles. It's as if there's no top or bottom to the world. Everything so dark—the pool, the sky, the walls of the cliffs surrounding the water's edge.

Suddenly I want to be nearer you. I see you bobbing in the water, and I swim in your direction. I splash your shoulders with the chill water. I am thinking how different you look from behind in the darkness in the pit.

You turn slowly to face me. It takes a moment for my brain to understand that it's not you at all.

The man is disfigured in a way I have never seen. Leaves grow from his face. His eyes are as bottomless as the pit itself, as bottomless as the sky.

He opens his mouth but no sound comes out. The space just getting wider and wider until the face disappears, and everything—water, trees, rocks, sky—is rushing into that abyss.

. . .

WHEN I WAKE, I put my hands to my face, expecting to feel leafy growths. There are only smooth planes, but it is not enough to return my pulse to normal or allow me any more sleep that night.

I suppose the dream was some kind of punishment for going where I should not go.

the mother

FOR THE REST OF THE TIME that Isabelle and Phillip were away I hardly spoke to you. Neither of us apologized for what had happened, but I hoped my silence would let you know I was not going to interfere again. And the softness of your voice made it clear you hadn't meant to hurt me, either.

I wouldn't have tried the spell at all if your nurse, Marie-Therese, hadn't stopped me in the kitchen one morning. I tried not to flinch when she took my hand and stared into my face as if I were a pool of water. She hadn't paid much attention to me before this.

"Ruby? Ruby is it?" She had a thick, slow Haitian accent.

I nodded. Isabelle had, of course, introduced us before they left. She was the woman I'd seen leaving the cottage the first night I'd come for dinner.

"You've got it, girl."

"What?"

"I'm not saying what isn't already known. You have to use it."

Then she walked away. She hardly spoke to me again after that.

THERE IS A STREAM DEEP in the forest. I hear it and smell it before I see it. The water is calling me. My head full of its whispers and green dampness.

I take off my shoes. I take off my cloak and drop it on the moist earth. In my pouch is a purple candle, a vial of rosemary oil, a large shell, a small, round earthenware vessel, and a bottle of purple paste I made with shells, dried herbs, and oils from Isabelle's shop. I anoint the candle with the rosemary oil and light it.

"Lady of the Forest, I need healing power for another, injured and weak. I seek you, Healing Mother."

I close my eyes and wait. I hear sounds, faint, strange. It seems to be the vibrations of the trees. When I open my eyes, I see sparkles, as if someone has tossed a handful of silver glitter into the air. A hazy form approaches and materializes, as she moves closer, into a tall, graceful woman with dark skin and flowing hair, a veil over her face. She stops and points to a grouping of rocks that form a shelf. The water pools there, then spills over the edge and joins the stream below. I find myself walking into the stream. My thin gown is soaked, so I stop and take it off. I stand naked, with my head bowed. The veiled woman is now holding the large shell filled with the purple paste. She dips her finger in the paste and begins to draw on my back. I feel the spiral motion of her finger. When she is finished, she takes the vessel and holds it under the running water. Then she pours the water over my back. It is warm, and the tension in my muscles dissolves. When I look at the water spilling off of me, I see that it is a poisonous yellow color.

I turn to ask the woman what is happening, but she is gone. There is the sound of leaves crunching and branches snapping behind me. A gray animal is running into the brush. I think the animal is a wolf. I take the vessel and fill it with water from the stream.

Suddenly I realize that I am cold.

I am standing naked in the middle of the forest, in the middle of winter, holding an urn of water and a shell filled with purple paste.

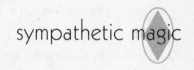

sympathetic magic

THE DAY WAS THE SAME as every other day. Marie-Therese came and went as usual, without a word, just those eyes watching me. When it was dark and the full moon had risen high above the cottage, I arranged the items on a tray and walked up the stairs very slowly, to the room where you slept. I put the tray on the small table near the window, where the moon's light touched it.

Your room looked different. There were pieces of cloth, covered with beads and sequins, spread across the furniture and over the windows. There were small jars with things floating inside of them—things I couldn't make out in the dim light. Candles were burning in each corner of the room. Marie-Therese had been working some spells of her own.

I anointed the candle I had brought and whispered the call as I lit the wick. Then I unrolled and spread a large piece of thin paper on the floor by your bedside. I dipped my finger into the jar of purple paste and traced the outline of a man's body on the paper. When it was finished, I began to draw the spiral in the center of the man's back. On the third loop, you stirred in your bed, and my hand froze as if you had seized it. I knew if you woke you'd be furious. This was so much riskier than reading a children's story. You might send me away and I'd never have another chance.

But you were still again.

I struggled to catch my breath and continued the spiral slowly, as tenderly as if I were actually touching you, all my energy focused on an image of you standing upright, fully healed. That was what healing was, I thought. Don't imagine the broken part at all. Only see the image of the whole. It is already whole because of your love. Love does not fragment.

There were strange tingling, burning sensations going up and down my arms, out my fingers, waves of energy flowing through my spine, down my legs and up to the top of my head. I finished the spiral and went back to the tray to get the water. I poured it over the image of the man. Watching the spiral bleed away, I imagined it was pain slowly dissipating. The sensations in my body were so strong now that I wondered if I was actually vibrating.

You cried out softly, a gasp, almost as if you were coming.

I'd never heard anything like that before. It came from somewhere so deep and hidden. I wanted to cry out with you. The vibrations were more intense in me now, coming faster and faster one after another.

Soon after that you whispered my name in your sleep. An icy wind battered the cottage, blowing clouds across the moon, and I was glad to be inside, basking at your bedside the whole night. Maybe it was the wind but I kept thinking I heard animals that night. Cats yowling as if they were in labor or dying or both, the scurrying feet of a frightened squirrel.

WE RETURN HOME from a restaurant dinner. A big storm is coming. The wind rages through the rooms when we open the front door. At the far end of the house, where Opal sleeps, we hear the window bang open and closed, panes of glass rattling. My father runs past us into her room.

The painting he gave her is on the floor in fragments. It is the image of a woman in a pink taffeta dress, reclining in front of a window. There is a letter on the floor beside her. Her face, pale with moonlight, looks distraught. I used to wonder what the letter said. Maybe it was from her lover.

It is a special gift, my father always reminds Opal, fragile, painted meticulously on glass. He only gives things like this to my sister, never to me. I never want them anyway, and when I see the broken pieces, I am gladder than ever that the painting wasn't mine.

But with the relief, comes guilt. Because I see the look in my father's eyes as he goes toward my sister who is cowering in the corner among shards of glass.

"You left the window open!"

There is the sound of crying, slamming, breaking, hitting all night. These are the words I remember my father screaming at my sister:

"Valuable!"

"Irreplaceable!"

How can he use those words about a thing, now, as he smashes his own child?

ISABELLE AND PHILLIP came home the next day. Isabelle dropped her bags at the doorway, ran to me, took my hands in hers, and looked into my eyes like a young girl searching for something precious she had lost.

"Is he much better, Ruby?"

I realized suddenly the magnitude of the hope they had attached to me. They had expected some kind of miracle and I had failed them. I couldn't meet Isabelle's eyes.

Just then, Marie-Therese came in from your room. I had never seen her smile before. It completely transformed her face. She put her arm around Isabelle's shoulders.

"There's something I think you should come and see."

THE MOONLIGHT WAS SHINING *through her dress, so he could see the woman's body beneath the fabric. He could see the outline of her high, round breasts and the darkness between her legs. She was standing at his side with a kitten perched on her shoulder. There were other cats, too, watching him from the shadows, and a squirrel in the branch of a tree. He didn't exactly see them but he knew they were there with her. Slowly he felt himself lifting and turning until he was floating on his stomach. He wondered how this could be, but he didn't question it for very long. He could smell the green, sodden scents of the forest, and the sweetness of melting wax, and the woman's fragrance, light and musky at the same time. Where was he? Where had she taken him?*

Her hands were on his back; that he knew. He could feel the gentle pressure of her fingertips and the cool thickness of some substance. Paint? She was tracing circular shapes around his spine, and wherever she touched, the warmth seemed to intensify, so even though it was night he could feel the sun.

Why did he get those bloody tattoos inked onto his lower back and abdomen? It was such an arrogant thing to do. As if he believed his body would stay young and strong forever. And then, just a few months later, he was an old man already, his spine smashed, sun broken. But he was feeling the heat now, from the woman. And it was spreading, deep into the skin, muscles, tendons. Deep to the bone. And then, as the cool water washed over him, he could feel his mind lighting up and his groin coming alive.

ALL HE COULD THINK *when he woke was how hungry he was. He hadn't felt hunger for months now. He had decided it suited him to be empty because that is how he was since the accident. Hollow. Like a smashed shell.*

Someone was always badgering him to eat. He simply remained silent until they gave up in frustration. Just as well, he had thought, they ought to know what it's like for me every day. Then he would feel guilty at making everyone as miserable as he was. Misery does not love company. Misery wants to be bloody left alone.

But this morning was different. He felt like he used to after swimming in the lake the first hot day of summer. Fresh. A layer of coolness evaporating off of his clammy skin.

Then he remembered seeing her in the gauzy gown and he felt something else he hadn't experienced in months. Desire. Was it a dream or had she really come into his room in the night?

sacrifice

MAMA CAT, STRANGE SQUIRREL, and Unnamed Kitten. For some reason, they were what I thought of that morning when I walked into your room and saw you completely changed.

CALEB DRAKE WAS A HOG FARMER with a snoutlike nose and skin so thick and leathery it was more like hide. He considered his healthy animals commodities and his sick ones liabilities—that was all. As for cats, they hardly existed as far as he was concerned, except to keep vermin off the property. He barely even fed them.

Caleb thought I was crazy but he indulged me anyway. I would come over every day to set food out for the cats.

Then I went looking for the youngest female, who I figured was probably easiest to tame. Eventually she did
come when I called, and let me pet her.

In the spring, she was getting round in the belly and
I knew she was pregnant. So I fed her a little food on the
side and kept an eye on the calendar. When she wasn't
around for a few days, I knew she must have delivered
and I had a feeling that something wasn't right. She was
such a small animal. I wandered around the barn calling
for her, but there was no response, so I went to the ma-
chine shed. After a few moments, I heard her. The meow
sounded urgent, and when I found her in the far corner, I
could tell she was relieved I was there. A kitten had gotten
stuck as she tried to birth him. I saw that he was dead.

I ran back to my house to get a box lined with an old
towel. Then I carefully transferred Mama Cat to the box,
her head resting on my hand. She fell asleep instantly. I
kept waking her the entire way to the vet's, telling her
not to die.

The vet shook his head when he saw her and asked
me if I was sure I wanted to do this.

I said, "How would you feel if that were you and no
one tried to help?"

I held her head while he removed the lodged kitten,
and she began purring with relief.

"Thank you," I said.

He shrugged. "She's thanking you."

I couldn't sleep all night. In the morning, the nurse called and told me that Mama Cat had died.

WHEN I WAS FOURTEEN, I babysat a little girl named Sasha. We'd go to the park every day from morning till evening and I'd make up elaborate games with her. She'd be the princess and I was the fairy godmother. The park gazebo was our castle, the swings were our flying chariots, and the slide our spiral staircase.

"You're so weird, Ruby!" she crooned to me one day, but I could tell by the wonder in her voice that she meant it as a compliment.

One morning, when we arrived, there was a group of older kids gathered around the gazebo. After a while, I saw a small animal of some kind on the ground in the middle of the pack. I told Sasha to stay on the swings while I went to investigate.

The kids had found a squirrel with a horribly misshapen back leg. The animal was full-grown and otherwise seemingly healthy, just slow-moving. I sent the kids away, scolding some and threatening to tell the parents of the ones I knew.

Sasha and I found a phone and I called animal control, because I knew the kids would be back. The lady who answered reassured me that she would find someone willing to take the squirrel for educational purposes and call me later.

At five o'clock, when I hadn't heard anything, I called them again. A man answered. He said the squirrel had been taken care of hours ago. I knew he meant killed. I was so enraged I could barely make any words come out of my mouth. The man seemed to find this amusing, so I hung up on him. I realized my hands were shaking with helplessness.

WHEN OUR CAT PADDY PAWS was pregnant with her kittens, I knew that I'd better make sure she didn't have them in the house. She was searching around for a cozy spot, but I was afraid my father would hurt her if she went into labor among his shirts. So I made her a box with lots of old towels and blankets and put it in the garage.

In the middle of the night, I didn't hear her cries but my father did. When I woke in the morning and went to check on Paddy, I found her and five kittens snuggled in the box. A couple of them were wet and one wasn't moving. I realized it had died.

My father had thrown a glass of water on Paddy Paws to make her stop crying.

I replaced the wet towels with dry ones and helped her settle in with her new family. Then I went to bury the dead kitten in the field behind our house.

My father had wanted to name Paddy Paws Jinx. I had refused; it seemed like a bad omen.

On my way out the door, my mother stopped me.

"Why don't you let Dad do that?"

I just gave her my most scathing stare and ran outside. My father never referred to what had happened or apologized for it. I didn't expect him to.

WAS THERE A CONNECTION between the dead animals and the way you had been transformed? I didn't know. But it was one way to make the loss worth something, at least in my mind. And that was where I still mostly lived.

spring

A MONTH AFTER YOUR PARENTS returned from their holiday, you rose from your bed and walked outside the door of the cottage. No one understood how this miracle had occurred. Marie-Therese had removed the beaded cloths, the candles, and the jars before Isabelle and Phillip came home. I had rolled up the paper with the outline of the man and hidden it underneath my bed where it remained all winter.

Now it was spring. I lay on my mattress in a fetal position with my eyes closed, breathing in the scent of blossoms on the wind, trying to become part of the air myself. I was not trying to be invisible. I was trying to re-member the springs of my childhood, to reassure myself that it had not all been trauma and dead creatures. The life I had made up was not that different from the life I really had. Was it?

Isabelle and I always talked about flowers. She told me their properties and essences and how to use them in spells, potions, and rituals. I told her things, too.

In the spring, where I grew up, red buds opened on the trees and lily of the valley filled the yard. At my grandparents' farm, the lilac bushes grew in dense purple clusters, so fragrant they made my knees weak. On May Day, my mother, Opal, and I woke at dawn, picked as many dew-speckled flowers as we could, and arranged them carefully in pastel construction-paper baskets we had made. Then we left them anonymously on people's doorsteps. I would get a ticklish feeling in my stomach; it was more exciting than Christmas morning for me to leave those baskets for people to find.

Everywhere I went, ladybugs attached themselves to my hair and clothes. "Good luck," my mother said. Sometimes she called me her little red ladybug. Opal and I ran outside after the rainstorms and stomped through the puddles in our yellow galoshes, soaking each other. When the sun came out, we hung the laundry on the line outside so our clothes would fill with the smell of the wind. The nights gurgled and hummed with the sound of locusts.

On the farm, there were some piglets whose mother had died and they wouldn't take their bottles; I asked my grandpa if I could try. I went into the pen and talked to the piglets and sang to them and fed them from bottles, like babies. I loved the suckling sounds and the tug of the bottle as their bodies wiggled with delight.

We had a big family picnic. There was barbecue pork to eat, and my father insisted I have some. He told me if I didn't I wouldn't get any dessert. I don't know if the meat was bad or if I was just sick from seeing that whole pig roasting on the spit and thinking of the suckling piglets. Either way, I threw up all night until I thought my body had turned all the way inside out, and I never touched pork again.

I DIDN'T TELL ISABELLE that last story; after all, she had a shop sign shaped like a sow. But the dead pig just sneaked into my mind. Turning and turning on its spit with its charred snout and cherry eyes. It was spring. Ask the poets. Not all demons look like men.

THIS MAY DAY, I filled a construction-paper basket with day lilies, sweet peas, daffodils, and daisies that I'd grown in the small plot Marge Bentley had let me tend. I left the basket on the doorstep of the cottage. As I crept away, the tickly feeling in my stomach was so strong it almost made me queasy.

Later, Isabelle called and invited me to the May Day festival. "A goddess was here at dawn with a basket of flowers. You must come see what she left." If a voice could wink, hers did.

At the fair, little girls in pastel dresses and hair ribbons and scrubbed little boys in starched white shirts, sky-blue vests, and short pants were dancing around, waving the Maypole ribbons.

"It's so beautifully pagan," Isabelle said.

You rolled your eyes. "Here they go."

"Well, it's just wonderful. How these things persist. The pole represents the sun god penetrating the earth goddess, Ruby. You probably could tell that."

"I hadn't really thought about it," I said. "Makes sense."

"It's also quite scientific," Phillip added. "The ancient Maypole sites have definite magnetic and energetic pulses readable by scientific equipment and perceptible to the very sensitive spirit."

We stood watching the children dance. Our arms weren't touching but I could feel your body's warmth and smell the soap you'd used that morning. Everyone was laughing and clapping, and my body swayed with the others' as if we were one. I almost could imagine that I was a spring goddess in the sleeveless white blouse and floral circle skirt I had made. I wished I could leap and twirl with the children and twist colored ribbons around the gleaming white pole.

As if in answer to my wish, several of the girls left the circle and started choosing people from the crowd to take their places. You pushed me forward as a girl with curly golden hair walked near us. I nearly knocked her over and she grabbed my hand. Her eyes were deep-set, blue, somehow very wise and serious in spite of her impish grin. She placed her ribbon in my hand and off I danced, leaping with the children. It was a relief to shamelessly express the joy inside my body. A ladybug landed on my arm and clung there. You were clapping and watching me twirl, and for a moment I felt that maybe you could love me. And I felt that maybe in that moment I was pure enough for your love.

the green man

I PACKED A PICNIC BASKET with hard-boiled eggs, apples
and grapes, cheese, delicate, buttery Mexican wedding
cookies, and a loaf of bread shaped like a woman's body,
from the funny bakery in town. We went down to the
meadow at the edge of the forest and found a spot under
a tree by a shallow creek where some wild blackberries
grew. It was the first time we had been out alone together.
The air was thin and the sky was a very sheer blue, as if
you could see through it to another place. Waxy daffodils had begun to open in the gardens, but in the meadow
the flowers were weedy and wind-blown.

   We were sitting together on the checked blanket
when you told me the story of your accident. You said

you hadn't told anyone yet, not coherently anyway, and I knew that this meant something—for you to have chosen me—so I held every word as if it was a kiss from your lips.

You said you had been in L.A. promoting your latest film and you were burned out, so burned out, you needed a break. It was the end of summer, and your mother kept saying how much she wanted you all to herself for a little while, so you swore your agent and publicist to secrecy and came home.

On your third day, you decided to take your horse, Day, for a ride. You hadn't seen her in ages and you thought it might do you both good to go out to the woods, bond a bit.

It was a gorgeous morning, the sunlight through the trees making a glimmering haze. And it was strange. You kept seeing animals. Not a few here and there, scurrying across the path, but groups of animals gathered in the shadows watching you. At first it was just small ones—chipmunks, squirrels, rabbits. But then there was a stag, a great big one, with an enormous rack, just standing by the edge of the path, staring at you. As you got closer, you kept expecting him to dash away but he was like a statue; for a minute, you thought he really was carved out of stone. But Day was getting nervous, snorting, whinnying, pawing the ground as she turned in circles on the narrow path. You were trying to calm her down, so you didn't notice at first, but then there was a feeling of electricity sparking the air, like just before a storm, and you looked over and someone was standing beside the stag.

THERE HAD BEEN STORIES of the leaf-faced man when you were a child, and you had nightmares about him, but you hadn't thought of him in years, you said. You said it was like some sign that you'd gone too far away from who you were, that the natural world was trying to warn you; you knew it sounded crazy but you couldn't explain it any other way. There he was, with his hand on the stag's back.

Nothing picturesque or magical about it, you said. The leaves were growing out of his flesh, forming his features like some kind of tumors, like they hurt him. And when you looked into his eyes, which were just spaces of darkness night caught in the leaves—you felt things you didn't understand. A terrible hollowness, you said, and other things you couldn't speak about.

THEN THE STAG REARED UP on his hind legs and Day couldn't take it anymore. She bolted. You dropped the reins and clutched her neck, just trying to hang on. She was jumping and thrashing through the trees and undergrowth. Everything was a blur, and the sound of branches snapping was amplified in your head. It was like screams, like crashing through disintegrating flesh and splintering bone.

"I woke two weeks later in hospital."

There were tears in your eyes and then I realized I was crying, too. I had watched the whole thing as you spoke, as if I were there, but behind glass, unable to do anything to stop it.

"I really want to ride her again, Ruby. I've never been afraid like this."

I said, "Let's go see her. Day. Let's go tomorrow. I know it will be all right."

A SHORT, STOCKY, middle-aged man greeted us.

"I've got her ready for you, Orion. I didn't know who Miss . . ."

"Ruby. Just Ruby." I held out my hand.

"Pleased to meet you Just Ruby. I'm Stuart. So why don't you have a look around, Ruby, and let me know which horse you fancy."

You had already gone over to a shadowy stall in the corner. I began to walk around the stable, stopping to stroke or whisper to the horses. The last stall was empty and I paused, turning to glance back at you, not wanting to interfere but trying to let you know I was there if you needed me.

Something tugged my braid, almost pulling me backward off my feet. I whirled around to see a large black horse, eyes glistening with mischief. He tossed his head and whinnied at me.

"Sorry, boy. I didn't see you there." I patted his neck.

Stuart came rushing over.

"It's all right, Stuart. We're just making friends."

"Well I'll be damned. Would you look at this? Orion look at this."

"What's the matter with you two?"

"She's met Night," Stuart said.

"This is Day's brother. My mother named them. She thinks it's witty. Day's like an angel, at least she was until . . . But Night's a little . . . difficult."

Stuart snorted. "That's an understatement."

"Stuart takes him out every now and then and Mum used to until he threw her."

"Well I'm going to ride him," I said. "You could use a good run, right boy? I take a Western saddle, please, Stuart."

Stuart raised his eyebrows at you and you hesitated, watching me stroke the horse's nose. Then you nodded and Stuart shrugged and went to get the saddle.

We waited at the stable doors. The scent of the meadows was already stronger now that the sun rose, and the sky was blue with a few scattered white clouds in the shapes of horses themselves. Stuart brought out the two animals. One was white, elegant, the other even more completely black and wild-looking in the sunlight. Day gazed disdainfully at her brother as I mounted him.

He felt spring-loaded. I pulled the reins taut and murmured to him. You were standing at Day's side, stroking her absently with one hand, the other in the saddle horn.

"It's all right," I said.

"You know, Ruby. This thing with my back. It can go at any second. I'll never know."

"If you don't want to do this, I understand," I said. "But if you do, I know it will be okay."

You pulled yourself up into the saddle and wheeled Day around to face me. You were smiling now, that daredevil grin. "I guess none of us ever knows, do we?"

"I'll bet you I can beat you to the edge of the forest," I shouted, letting the restless animal do what he was meant to.

"Amazing."

You pulled up to the dark cluster of trees a split second after me. The horses stopped easily here; even Night seemed slightly unsure.

"What's amazing?" I laughed. "That I beat you? Or being out with your girl again?"

"Well that. But I meant you. On that horse."

"Sometimes a wild horse needs to feel that his rider is just a little bit wilder," I said. Ruby on the ground might not have said it but Ruby in the saddle could say almost anything at all.

You arched one eyebrow.

"Are you ready?" I asked, smoothing out the ridges along Night's wide neck.

You nodded, your jaw set, and I could tell you were remembering the last time you rode among these trees. Or imagining the last time you left them.

The path was just wide enough for us to go side by side, the earth swollen with moisture from the spring rains. As the growth became denser, the ground felt firmer; the giant trees had already sucked up all the wetness.

We rode in silence, just listening. Then you stopped and pointed.

There, in the trees, was a child-sized house made entirely of vines. A tree stump was on either side of the door and the first blooms of lily of the valley surrounded the walls. The doorway and windows were void of light, and somehow the contrast between that darkness and the bright white flowers disturbed me.

I thought of the painting my mother's mother had in her house when I was a child. It was a dark hillside with a small arched wooden door built into it. A dirt road wound up from the door behind the hill and into a thick wood where the trees were so dark green they appeared almost black.

I remembered asking my grandmother about it. I don't think she ever told me much, but whenever I thought of the painting, I recalled another conversation we had had, about how she used to hold séances with her mother and aunts when she was a child. How they levitated a table once. They had learned this from their mother, who had been a circus performer. Even in her eighties, my great-great-grandmother would dress up in a sari, paint her eyes with black kohl, lie across the back of two chairs, and insist that her husband and his brothers lift her in the air.

The painting frightened me, but in a pleasant way. My eyes watered and my chest tightened with excitement. I liked to imagine that the house belonged to a witch and that I was going to take the dirt path, march right up to her door, and knock.

"I guess magic isn't always good," you said.

"What? I'm sorry."

"All right, dreamy. I was telling you about the house."

"And the magic?"

"I played here when I was a kid. We used to come and wait for something fantastic to happen but my mother told me to be careful what you wish for."

Magic isn't always good. What had you meant by that? I tried to rub away the goose bumps on my arms, and then I followed you down the path away from the vine house.

"There was a place like this in the woods where I grew up. A steamboat, just standing there among the trees, completely overgrown with moss and vines. I have no idea how it got there. I used to play there all the time but most of the other kids were too spooked by it. Inside it was so dark and musty, with these amazing little rooms."

You looked back at me, cocking your head. "You're really something, Ruby. I try to impress you but you keep topping me. What are you, some kind of miracle-worker?"

Then, silence. I couldn't see your face, but somehow I could tell you were remembering what you'd said to me at Christmas.

You pulled Day over to the side of the path and faced me. "I'm sorry, Ruby. I never apologized. I was just so frightened I wouldn't be able to move or do anything again."

"I'm the one that should have apologized."

"No, all you did was try to help me. You did help me."

It felt like too much. I looked away and we kept riding then, not speaking. All of a sudden I heard you murmur: "Bloody hell."

"What?"

"We passed it. The spot where it happened. We went right by it and I didn't even notice."

The way you were looking at me, your eyes wide, your lips slightly parted, I could tell you thought it was more magic. I wanted to tell you that I didn't really know what I was doing. I was just like my grandmother as a little girl, calling on ghosts and lifting tables with her fingertips. Not really understanding any of it but ready to knock on the witch's door anyway.

Instead of replying, I turned Night around and started back to the stable. When we reached the edge of the woods, we broke into a gallop. You and the horses and I—part of the wind.

Stuart was waiting for us, squinting, stamping down straw with his boots. He seemed relieved.

"Didn't give you any trouble then, Miss?" he asked me.

"Oh no, Orion was a perfect gentleman." I winked at him. Then I slid off Night's back and patted the horse's powerful neck. "And Night was, too."

You grinned at me as we walked back to the car.

"I'm famished," you said. "Let's cook a meal with everything in the house."

lady of the forest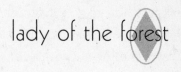

AFTER CLEARING UP THE DISHES from dinner, I called your name but you didn't answer. I looked in every room but you weren't anywhere. I felt panicky. Not that you could have gone anywhere. Not that something could be wrong. Where were you? Orion?

I passed the door leading to the back garden and heard your voice calling my name. I ran out onto the soft grass. The night smelled sweet. All of a sudden, everything was soft and sweet and warm. You were sitting on a blanket in the middle of the garden, where the ground rose to a soft mound, perfect for stargazing.

"I couldn't find you." I felt so stupid for letting you see my fear.

"I'm sorry. I didn't mean to worry you."

When I didn't move, you said my name. I still didn't know how to go to you. Then you reached out your hand.

There is no possible way I can ever refuse you, your eyes pulling me with a constantly questioning gaze, your lips always teasing me, the way they never quite meet in the center. That opening holds every hope poised right there. And when you speak, every cell of my body resonates with the sound.

I walked to you, never taking my eyes from your face. I sat next to you and you lay back, pulling me so my head was resting on your shoulder. The stars were so bright they seemed to be laughing.

"There you are," I said, pointing up to the sky. I had looked up the myth in one of Isabelle's books. Your namesake was a powerful hunter who was blinded by a king when Orion wooed his daughter. Orion's sight was restored by Dawn, who had fallen in love with him. But then Artemis slew him with her arrows. He was too beautiful to die and became a constellation.

"When I found out the myth behind it, I asked my mother why she would choose that. She said, 'We have to start using the lovely old names or they will go to waste. We just have to make up a new mythology. You'll do that.'"

"Big responsibility."

You rolled your eyes. "She is convinced I'm meant for a life of mythic proportions."

"Well it looks like she's right."

You angled your face to look down at me. I could feel your breath moving the tiny stray hairs on my forehead. "I don't know about me. You're the one. What is it with you and these animals, Ruby? Where do you come from?" Your eyes were like a horse's, so large and dark, full of the reflected world.

I told you, "I had a horse when I was twelve. Vixen. She was what they call high-spirited, but really she was just wild. She threw me once and cracked my ribs. But I just kept getting back on her."

That was all I told you about my experiences with animals.

"Ruby, thank you for going riding with me. I couldn't have done it yet without you there."

I lowered my face so that we were nearly touching noses. Neither one of us closed our eyes. I touched my lips to yours, brushing them gently. Then I kissed you, deep and full.

WE HAVE AN ALFALFA FIELD behind our house. One spring after it is mowed and bailed, we find a nest of four baby rabbits. Their mother lies dead nearby, mangled by the machinery. Opal and I take them home in a box, and Mr. Becker gives us a huge cage and tells us how to care for them. He comes over regularly to check on them and give them shots. I feel so proud when he tells us how healthy and tame they have become.

My father starts getting upset though. He says we have to get rid of them or he is going to make stew. We stand in front of the supermarket for days trying to give them away. All but three are taken, but no one wants the littlest one, whose name is Peter. I lie awake at night, so scared that my dad is going to cook him. I pray to the Lady of the Forest to help us.

Walter-Mae Livingston lives at the edge of town in a large, ramshackle house with a greyhound she had saved from being put down when it could no longer race, a blind white German shepherd, and a three-legged cat. People say Walter-Mae is a witch, and the kids all run away when she comes to town to buy her groceries.

I march up to her door one day with Peter in a box. She asks me in and shows me her family. The two dogs and the cat are all eating together out of the same bowl. Walter-Mae shows me the bed where they all sleep together, too.

"Please take Peter," I say. "I'm afraid my dad will eat him."

"Who's your daddy?" she asks. Her green eyes look brighter in contrast to her skin, like a black cat's. I even imagine that the pupils are elongated. She seems to be seeing straight through my skull into my brain.

I shake my head. "It doesn't matter. Please, just take him."

When I come back to check on Peter three weeks later, he is eating and sleeping with the greyhound, the shepherd, and the three-legged cat. Maybe Walter-Mae Livingston really is a witch. Or an angel, or the Lady of the Forest I had sent my prayers to. I always wanted to be like her.

DAD COMES HOME from work early. I haven't yet fed our dog, Buford. Dad starts screaming at me. He takes Buford downstairs to the basement and locks him in. Then he comes back up. I'm just standing there, putting the dog's food in his bowl to take down to him. My father comes up behind me and grabs my arm. He drags me to the top of the staircase and kicks me so I stumble down. Then he leaves. I go in to Buford. He doesn't even want his food. He lies down on his bed and I lie down with him, my head on his chest, listening to his heartbeat.

Later that day, we all leave for my grandparents' farm. But Dad won't take Buford—we always take him. He throws him into the kitchen and puts up the gate. I guess he's still punishing us both.

Buford doesn't forget what happened. He breaks out of the kitchen. When we get home, we see he has pulled one pillow off of the bed and peed on it. It's Dad's pillow.

I think Dad is going to kill Buford but instead they just stare at each other. I've never seen an animal look like that. At least not a domestic one. My father just walks away after a while. But I know he'll find some way to punish. It never just ends. It's got to go somewhere.

One day, I am standing in the kitchen setting out jelly beans in pastel paper-cup cake-pan liners for my birthday party. Cake and ice cream and party favors, balloons and presents and jelly beans. I even got a kitten as a present from my mom. I call her Batgirl. She's black, with huge green eyes. Sunshine through the window and the kitten is sleeping. Nothing bad can happen.

All of a sudden, my father comes into the house, almost running. I hear the china in the cabinet rattle. He is screaming about how I missed a speck of cat shit on the lawn mower seat when I cleaned it. He punches me in the arm. My new kitten is cowering in the corner, watching.

The next day, I go out the back door to find Batgirl. I am carrying her food in a little yellow bowl.

She's dead, lying on the back step, blood oozing from her mouth and nose. It is never discussed but I know who killed her.

Three stories. In the first, I saved the animal, in the second, he helped me. In the last story, neither of us could be saved.

WHEN I PULLED AWAY, your eyes were surprised and you were smiling that amused, slightly cocky smile. I felt my face flush and I was glad for the darkness. What had I just done? I jumped to my feet, shoving my hands awkwardly into the pockets of my jeans.

"I'm sorry, Orion. I'm really sorry. You must think I'm such an idiot."

"That's not what I was thinking at all. I was thinking what an amazing mouth you have."

I turned and went back into the house. You stopped me at the front door. You were still smiling.

"Why did you do that?" you asked.

I wished I could perform the invisibility spell. "I already said I was sorry. What else do you want?"

The smile was gone now. "Ruby, that's not what I meant. Why did you walk away from me?"

I tucked my hair behind my ears and looked at my shoes, the way I used to do when I was little. "I'm sorry.

I was just so shocked at myself. For doing that. And I was afraid . . ."

You interrupted me. "There is one thing I want you to know. You never have to be afraid of me in any way." I glanced up and saw you standing there looking at me, eyes darkened with concern. "And please stop apologizing. When we look back on our first kiss I don't want us to remember it as sorry."

I brushed your cheek with my lips and ran out into the night.

the maiden

I STOP AT THE EDGE of the forest. The darkness is so deep that I imagine I can see my own reflection in it. The moon is waxing, but the sky is full of a rolling fog that blocks any light. I shiver in the cloak Isabelle had made me, drink the potion from the blue glass bottle, look up at the sky, and say the words from the book of spells.

"Love has led me and now I must follow. Gentle Maiden, sister moon, show me the path to my desire."

The words sound strange, old-fashioned, but I repeat them anyway, until they begin to feel part of me.

I close my eyes and cross into the darkness.

When I open my eyes again, I see a path winding among the trees, lit by tiny flying lights. They twirl and dance, hovering one minute and darting the next, staying just far enough ahead that I can't really see them clearly. The smells of roses, jasmine, lily of the valley grow stronger with each step I take over the springy pine needles.

The path opens to a clearing where the trees form a structure, some kind of multiroomed gazebo. The entrance is covered with what appears to be a gauzy cloth, but when it touches my face, I see that it is really a thin veil of moss. Inside the gazebo are chaise longues and chairs covered in peach, rose, and pale yellow silks and velvets, heaped with pillows of soft green and blue. The twinkling lights from the path gather around the edges of the ceiling that is open to the sky. In the center of the room is a small blossoming tree that holds in its branches a basin filled with water. A breeze stirs the water releasing the scent of roses. I feel warm and tingling, high with it.

Someone is here with me; I can feel her presence. I turn to see a young woman standing in the doorway. She is about my own age, maybe a little younger, with moonlike skin and long, silky, golden ringlets full of tiny pink blossoms that look as if they have sprouted there. Her dress seems to change color as she moves and the light hits it in different ways.

I smile at her cautiously and she reaches out her hand to me.

I pull back with shock as soon as I feel her skin: desire surges through me, from my core, out my limbs to my fingers and toes.

She reaches out to touch one of the flowers on the small tree, then gestures for me to do the same. I hesitantly graze the petal with my fingertip. The sensation of wanting fills my body again, just as it had begun to ebb. I touch the rose water in the basin and every one of my cells reverberates with more sensation.

I follow the girl to one of the day beds but it is hard to walk with so much blood pounding through me. She lies back on the bed and I sit at the edge of it.

My whole body relaxes as if invisible hands are massaging me. I close my eyes, and when I open them, I see Orion reclining beside me where the girl was. He tosses his dark curls out of his eyes and stretches his limbs. I can see the shadow of hair on his strong chin, the way his delicate nostrils move when he breathes, the thickness of his eyelashes, the motion of his Adam's apple. Tears prick like pins at the inner corners of my eyes. I want him so much. Why do I want him so much? I don't even know him.

The girl—herself again—stands and puts her hands on my temples. They start to throb. I feel like my brain is contracting and expanding. I want to scream. I'm not sure if it's desire or sadness or fear.

Suddenly, the girl changes again. Her ringlets straighten out into smooth strands, still blond, and her clothes transform into jeans and a jean jacket over a pink tank top. She has on blue eye shadow and lip gloss and she is chewing bubble gum. She smells of sugar and cigarettes.

"You know, someone told me that virgin didn't used to mean you didn't have sex with anyone. It just meant you didn't have a husband. You could sleep around as much as you wanted."

"Tiger?" I say. "Tiger Smokler?"

"Hey, Ruby."

"What are you doing here?"

"I'm here for you," she says. "You can't leave where you come from."

Then she gets up and walks out of the gazebo.

I follow her.

I CAME BACK AND COLLAPSED on my bed. What was happening to me? I wondered. Had I finally gone completely mad? Three times they had happened, but none of these episodes in the forest could be real.

the dreams

WHEN I WAS A LITTLE GIRL, I had four dreams. I told my mother and my sister and we always talked about them, how strange they were, how vivid and cinematic and terrifying. They became part of the family legend, Ruby's Dreams, like the time I saw King and Queen walking on the hill. But the problem was—the thing I never told my family—the dreams weren't dreams at all.

I AM FOUR YEARS OLD. I wake from a deep sleep. A woman is standing in the door of my bedroom. She is ghostly white—her long, stringy hair, her skin, her long nightgown with the elastic bands around her trembling wrists—but solid in form, dark eyes ringed with circles, sinking into loose folds of flesh.

I know she is here to hurt me. I know I need to fight. I get up and throw my little yellow plastic chair at her. It hits her and she glares at me, baring her teeth. Then she is gone.

The next morning I tell my mother. I tell her everything except the first part. The waking-up part.

I AM SEVEN YEARS OLD. I'm in my bed and wake suddenly. I hear something coming down the hall. I sit up, gripping the sheets over my heart as if I'm trying to keep it from escaping my body. At the foot of the bed are two smallish men crawling on their knees. I can just see the tops of their heads, level with the mattress. Slung between them, resting on their backs, is a pole and tied to it a wolf, all four feet bound together. The men regard me with surprised faces as if I am the nightmare. We all stare at each other for a moment. The wolf's eyes are woeful.

I think, I am the wolf, I am the moon, I am the dark of the night.

Why am I so afraid of the darkness?

I don't see the men and the wolf anymore. I see my mother lying on her back on the floor, her wrists pressed together as if they are bound. She is weeping.

. . .

TEN YEARS OLD. I'm walking down the long dirt rock road that leads to town from our house. To my right is a big open pasture for cows. To the left is a trailer court. The flimsy trailers look depressing, but people have tried to make them more inviting with plastic flowers in window boxes, ceramic ducks and gnomes, cheap lace curtains, and Christmas lights. I am thinking of Tiger Smokler. She and her brothers all looked like Southern California surfers. They were so blond and miraculously tan, even in the winter, with really white teeth. When Tiger committed suicide, her family lost their house and moved into one of those trailers. Later, her parents divorced and her mom started drinking. Tiger's brothers rode my bus. Bad boys, people said. They seemed nice to me, though. I always wanted to talk to them, even just say hello, but I never did.

I look into the sky at the enormous clouds. They part. I stand there, staring up, wanting to call for someone else to see but I can't speak.

A girl is bound and gagged, tied to a post. A man is standing over her, brandishing a knife. He is bearded and very thin, wearing only a loincloth. There are bloody marks on his palms and feet.

"Wait!" I yell. "What are you doing?"

He looks at me calmly and raises the knife.

"Tiger?" I scream.

The clouds close again and I run toward home as a light rain starts to fall.

THAT SAME YEAR. I am in the kitchen with my mom, helping her make meatloaf. I see something odd outside in the distance and go onto the deck to get a better view. A house on the edge of town is on fire, flames leaping from the windows. I'm yelling to my mom, "Fire, fire, call the fire department!" but she can't hear me. I see her through the glass, wrist-deep in raw meat, eyes wet with onion tears. I look back at the house. As I watch, the fire jumps to the roof of the church next door. The house looks untouched. Out of the church's flaming roof I see something. It's a large fierce bird and it's flying straight at me. I back away from the edge of the deck, startled by the colorful span of wings. The bird lands on the top rail of the deck and looks at me, cocking its head questioningly. I can hear its thoughts in my mind.

"I love you," the bird is telling me. "I would like to stay with you awhile."

Later, I discover the name of the bird. It is not in a

book about animals but a book of mythology. Rising from the flames. Phoenix.

. . .

MAYBE I AM CRAZY. Or maybe something else happened in my bedroom, in the kitchen in the fields by the trailer park. Something that could not be remembered. Something unforgivable.

the knowing

WE WENT OUT FOR INDIAN food at a tiny restaurant with purple and saffron-colored walls. We ate saag palu, the spinach just melting with ghee, and creamy, spicy cauliflower-and-potato alu gobi. Wrapping everything in the garlic naan so that the textures and flavors blended together. Our eyes were watering from the spices and we tried to cool off with the cucumber-and-yogurt raita. I looked at you sipping your wine.

"I would give anything to be that wine in your mouth," I said.

"I wish you were this wine in my mouth." You leaned over and pressed your lips to mine. They burned with the spices. My whole body was burning.

"Let's go dancing," you said.

A little band was playing salsa music at the pub. You put your hand on my lower back and I moved my hips slowly. You pressed against me and I felt your chest, your heartbeat, your pelvis.

"Where did you learn to dance like this?" you asked.

I smiled into your neck.

"Where did you come from? I'm serious, Ruby. I've never met anyone like you."

WE CAME BACK FROM DANCING and I fell into the sofa, my yellow flowered skirt spreading out around my legs. I felt the summer breeze through the cottage windows. We were laughing. I can't even remember why. We were just laughing because we were together.

The laughter stopped. You were standing across the room with two glasses of wine but you set them down as if you had forgotten about them. You moved over to me very slowly and kneeled in front of me. Your eyes stayed on my face as you put your hands on my ankles and ran them up my legs. You looked down, then back up at me, asking.

I couldn't breathe. My mouth was parted slightly and I felt a gentle, stinging sensation on my lips.

You glided your hands along the tops of my thighs

under my skirt, stopping just at the place where my legs met my hips. I was sweating there. You looked back into my eyes and kissed me very softly with your whole mouth. When I kissed you I could smell myself. I didn't smell like a girl. I smelled like a meadow in the sun. But then I pulled away from you. I wanted to see your face again.

We were both out of breath and your pupils were dilated so your eyes looked black, like a horse's, like Night's. You ran your hands up my torso and I arched my back, driving my breast into your hand. We were both burning up. The thin fabric of my clothes felt heavy and hot. You began to undo the buttons of my blouse and I moved my shoulders so it slipped off. Then I pushed you back and stood up, sliding my skirt off. When you pulled your shirt over your head, I gasped out loud without meaning to. I had never seen anything as perfect as that torso. And there was the sun tattooed on your abdomen. Blazing, burning me. I reached out, trembling, and lightly touched the very center of that sun. I looked up and saw the same sun burning in your eyes.

You took my hand and pressed it full and flat against your chest. With your other arm you drew me to you.

"Is this too soon?" you whispered.

Was it too soon? Of course not. This is all I had ever wanted. Wasn't it? Then why did I want to run? What was I afraid of?

But it was too late to answer. Your mouth was covering mine while you unfastened my bra and pressed your body to me so my nipples pierced your chest, answering your question. As if they already knew my body inch for inch, your hands slid down my waist and pushed my panties off my hips. They were soaking wet with the rest of your answer.

You stopped kissing me and loosened your hold for a moment. I still had one more chance. I am Ruby, I told myself, named for the stone that chases away evil spirits. But what demons would be released if I stopped fighting against them, even for a moment?

I'D ALWAYS HAD A KNOWING. I'd know things when I entered a room, know things before they happened, know things I shouldn't know.

And there was the worst knowing. That day. Because the hairs stood up on the back of my neck and I knew, I knew but I couldn't stop it from happening.

I AM TWELVE. Summer vacation. My mom tells me that she and Opal will be gone most of the day. I am to stay home and clean the bathroom, set out and clean up my dad's lunch.

My father, who works in a completely different town, never comes home for lunch.

I eat my cheese sandwich and go into the bathroom to clean. I lock the door. I don't know why. *Something wicked this way comes*, I think. But it doesn't make a difference.

I hear him come in the back door. A few moments pass while I sit there on the floor, holding the toilet brush, smelling the chemicals. There isn't enough air in here, I think. I should open a window. But I don't.

There's a knock on the door.

I don't answer.

The doorknob jiggles. Then the question:

"Why's the door locked?"

"Oh, just habit, I guess." My voice sounds like someone else's. Someone who doesn't know. Someone who is only surprised.

From behind the door: "Well, unlock it."

I do what he says. He is standing there with his pants down and an erection.

He is smiling.

He leads me from the bathroom to the bedroom floor. He leads someone. Not Ruby. Where is Ruby? Ruby,

named for the jewel that is thought to glow darker when
illness is coming or the owner is in danger.

All I remember after that is his voice.

"I'm teaching you. What is okay to let a boy do or
not do to you."

When he is finished, this is what happens:

He eats the lunch I made for him and leaves.

I finish cleaning my bathroom.

When my mother and sister return and ask why I am
crying, I tell them I got bathroom cleaner in my eye. The
stuff that smelled so bad, you know? I thought I was
protecting them by not telling them.

A FEW DAYS LATER, when he is having one of his tan-
trums, Mom insists that I go downstairs into the basement (there is always, in every house we move into, a
basement) and watch TV with him after dinner.

"No," I say. I am Ruby again.

She threatens to ground me for two weeks. There is a
school dance coming up that I will miss.

I glare at her. I can feel my eye sockets burning with it.

"If you knew everything you wouldn't make me go
down there with him," I say.

My mother named me for a precious stone. One that
opens the heart to love, grows darker when the owner is

in danger or illness is coming, chases away evil spirits. I know she loves me. I know she doesn't want to hurt me.

That same mother never asked me. She never asked me what I meant.

The second attempt. A few weeks later. Middle of the night. I fight. Mom is sleeping just across the hall. He gives up, hits me, and leaves.

Third and final attempt. Five years later. Different town. Different house. Another basement. My sister is away at school, so her room is not the one at the most remote part of the house.

Mine is.

It is the middle of the night again. I fight and fight. He's really angry. Too bad. I don't care what happens. He's not doing it again.

He gives up, cursing. He doesn't hit me this time. I tell him he's never going to win. I'll never let him do that to me ever again.

IT IS THE SMALLEST TOWN we have lived in, the most removed and the least sophisticated. Now I understand why he chose it.

At school the next day I have an appointment with the counselor. He looks at me with this pity that makes me sick to my stomach. I don't want pity, his or anyone else's. I can tell he doesn't know what to do with me, so he sends me back to class.

It is in the middle of an algebra test when they come for me—the counselor and two police officers. They take me to the jailhouse, to the room where they question accused criminals. I suppose they are trying to scare me in case I am lying. They question me with a psychologist for two hours. Then they bring my mother in.

She sits across the table from me. The look on her face is disbelief mingled with fear. She asks me if I am telling the truth or if I am just angry at Dad for something.

"Oh, yeah, Mom, I get my jollies out of making up horror stories for the police. You don't believe me? Well let me think. I'll give you an example. Do you remember that time you forced me to go downstairs with Dad and I told you you wouldn't make me if you knew everything?"

She turns the color of sheets. I have heard that expression before but I have never seen it. We always bleach the sheets in our house.

My mother and I are taken to the county courthouse where my father is waiting. He is in the judge's office. Why didn't they have him in handcuffs? He cries and says he is sorry. He wants to hug me but I recoil. Then they send him home with Mom and I am put in a foster home where I stay for three weeks I don't remember much about those weeks. I just kept wondering, why am I the one who is being punished?

Opal calls. She is away at college in the next town, and when my mom told her what happened she didn't say anything. But now she wants to talk. She wants us to come see her.

When we get to her apartment, she is wearing her nightgown and squatting over the heater, the way she and I used to do on cold nights when we were little. She is mumbling and rocking back and forth. My mother and I sit down on the floor too, and my mother puts her arms around her. I don't wish that my mom would do that for me. Somehow I understand that Opal needs more comfort than I do now.

"What is it?" I say finally. "You have to tell us everything."

Opal tells us that it has been going on since she was ten years old. She tells us about the time he "taught" her to play tennis and the time in the basement and the time in the bathroom and the time in the middle of the night. Something is familiar about each one, and I realize that Opal has told me these stories before, but they were about her and boys from high school or college. Then she tells us about how before she moved away she finally put a lock on her door in the house we live now. Her old bedroom is in the basement. He took the doorknob off. She put another lock on and barricaded the door with a heavy wooden dresser. He took the door off its hinges.

"I wanted to protect you, Ruby," Opal says. "I believed that if I didn't tell anyone he wouldn't hurt you. I just wanted you to be safe."

I thought I had fought him my whole life and now I know that I have deceived myself. But he is not going to win. We go back to the judge and file a report.

The judge takes me aside and says under his breath, "Ruby, are you aware of what you are saying? Do you know the severity of these charges?"

He ends up dropping every charge against my father. It is only later that I think about why my father was in the judge's office that day, what he was doing, how he was bargaining. My father, the banker.

I am allowed to go back to my mother. We move into an apartment. My father stays in the house.

Opal drops out of school and Steven helps us move her in with her boyfriend even farther away. We never let my father know where she is.

It is over. But in some ways it isn't.

. . .

THE SUN DIDN'T ONLY kiss me. I refused to wear sunscreen. I lay out under him for so long that he seared my skin. Blistered bubbled up. The burns were so bad that we had to get cream from the emergency room, the kind for burn victims, not worshipers.

WE WERE LYING in the bathtub together. You got out, wrapped a towel around your hips, and left the room. When you came back, you had your camera. I resisted the impulse to cover my body, hide under the bubbles. Your Ruby would not do this. Your Ruby would smile and lie back, enjoying your eyes on her, enjoying the water, the bubbles, the warmth, the feeling of being watched.

You snapped some pictures and then knelt beside the tub.

"Ruby, there's something I have to talk to you about."

I smiled at you but the knowing was starting. I pushed it away.

"I have to go on location. I got a movie. It's because of you! They can't believe how I've recovered and it's because of you. I don't want to leave you but I have to go. Maybe you could come visit me there, in L.A., when I'm settled. It would be so great to have you there."

Those are not the actual words you said. But that was

the idea. I hardly heard you. All I could think was that you were leaving. And you didn't know who I was.

When I was five years old, my dad took my picture when I was getting out of my bathtub.

"Look at that body," he would say. "Ugly already."

I was five years old.

I want to smash Orion's camera lens. I want him to leave. I am not Orion's Ruby.

my father always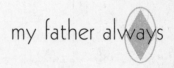

AFTER ORION LEFT, Isabelle and Phillip were kinder than ever to me. Isabelle said she needed me to spend more time at the shop, although there were very few customers. She invited me over for dinner every night and talked about all sorts of things—flowers and baking and spells for abundance but never about her son.

Phillip wanted to talk to me about writing. He asked how it was going and if he could help me in any way. I thanked him but I didn't want to get too into it; I didn't want him to find out what I had been working on.

"Maybe you'd like a few exercises?" he said. "My students enjoy them."

One of the exercises Phillip suggested was to fill in the rest of the sentences "My father always . . ." and "My mother never . . ." He said that when he used this in a writing workshop, the students read their work through their sobs; it was very effective, he said.

"I had Orion do it once," he told me. "As a kind of therapy, really, more than anything."

It was the first time he'd mentioned his son to me since he'd left; I knew that Phillip, like Isabelle, was being protective of my feelings.

I tried not to show any emotion on my face.

"He said, 'My father never was my father and my mother always thought it was all right to lie.' He was very angry at us at the time, obviously."

Then Phillip told me the story of how he and Isabelle had conceived their son when she was married to the man Orion believed to be his father.

"It took him a long time to forgive us," Phillip said. "Sometimes I'm not sure if he has, completely. It's made him very sensitive to any kind of untruth or betrayal." Phillip paused, watching me, as if he were deciding how much to share, how much I needed to hear to feel reassured. Unfortunately, it didn't reassure me at all.

"That's why he feels so strongly about you, Ruby. He trusts you more than anyone, I believe."

It was hard to hide the wincing; all my body parts seemed to be contracting with shame.

Everything was a lie. There was no way I could even share the answers to the exercise with Phillip, let alone Orion.

MY FATHER ALWAYS had his hand in his pants. Whatever he was doing—talking on the phone, watching television, having a beer—he'd absently be playing with himself. No one ever told him to stop. It made me sick to my stomach. When I told a school counselor about it once, she said it was normal, just something men do. She didn't ask any more questions.

My father always chose homes with basements.

My father always screamed and threw things.

My father always abused animals.

My father always put my sister in the room farthest from the rest of the rooms.

My father always raped her.

MY MOTHER NEVER asked questions.

My mother, who had two girls more precious to her than any jewels, more precious to her, she said, than her own life, never forgave herself for not protecting them.

. . .

I HAD FORGIVEN HER but I never would forgive my father.

If I were to be truthful, as, Phillip said, all writers must be, I always wanted to see the man dead.

threefold

BY THE TIME I'D FOUND THE SPELL I was looking for, the
candles I'd lit were only inches above their holders and
the room was filled with the smell of pooling beeswax.
My eyes were aching down to the sockets and my mind
felt muddled with all the incantations I had read in the
huge old leather-bound book without a title, only the
tree of life embossed on its cover. But I had found what
I wanted: "Harnessing the Fates." Strangely, it had a star
drawn beside it and the words "black wooden box with
silver fasteners, corner bookcase, third shelf." I recognized Isabelle's elegant hand.

The box was where she had said it would be. I wondered why Isabelle had this potion already prepared.

Then I noticed some more of her writing on the page beneath the spell. It was as if she had heard my question and was answering.

"This is to be used only in the most dire circumstances. Crafter: remember the threefold law!"

I had read about this before in other witchcraft books. It meant that the spell and its intentions would come back three times stronger upon the one performing it.

Now that Orion was gone, I didn't care anymore. I would accept whatever came to me. I would pay the price.

I slipped the bottle of potion into my pocket and, holding the leather-bound book like a baby, I left Isabelle's shop and was enveloped by the night.

It felt so natural for me to be wrapped in a dark cloak on my way to this forest that I wondered if I had done it in another life. And had Orion and Isabelle been part of that life? Of course I knew about reincarnation, but Isabelle had told me about something else—"soul circles," when a group of people continue to find each other again and again. That thought gave me confidence as I neared the edge of the woods.

I came to a small circular clearing about half a mile in through the dense growth. That is where I set up my altar with the objects in my pack. I lit the bundle of dried sage, held it above my head and spun slowly clockwise three times, spiraling out to the circle's edge. Then I moved the sage around my body, also three times. Was it that easy to purify myself? With a bunch of dried leaves and smoke?

I extinguished the burning sage in a small cauldron on my altar and set out the quarter candles. Green for north, red for south, yellow for east, blue for west. I lit each one and then, in the candle flames, lit the four sticks of incense I had brought. The smell was all the elements combined, not only the minerals of earth and the smoke of fire but water and wind.

I stood in the center of the circle, my feet spread apart and firmly planted, and raised my athame staff to the sky. Then I lowered it and pointed it at the ground at the east quarter. I moved to the yellow candle and walked slowly around the circle, ending where I had begun. I returned to the altar and placed my athame's wooden tip into the salt, then the water, blessing them. I mixed three pinches of salt into the water, stirring three times after each addition. Again I moved around the circle, sprinkling the water as I went. I repeated this with incense, waving the stick so the smoke curled up into the air. My circle was cast.

I moved to each quarter with my athame in my right

hand and drew the pentagram with its tip. Then I lowered my right hand, pointed it at the quarter candle, raised my left hand toward the east, and received the element. I did this for each quarter and returned to the center of my circle. I took out the potion and held it above my head.

"Fates, join me in my circle and bless me with your power. I am fearless and will do your bidding. My eyes are your eyes, my hands are your hands, my heart your heart."

I consumed the fiery liquid in one gulp, shuddering as I felt it burn through my body. The spell book told me that next I must walk "widdershins" around the perimeter of the cast circle. Like everything else that night, this did not seem strange. The soul I had once been and the person I was becoming knew to walk counterclockwise. The Ruby who had lived in her father's house had ceased to exist.

AS I WALK, I SEE a few drops of water bubbling out of the ground in the center of the circle. They come faster and faster until a clear, shallow pool forms, with flowers growing around it that I hadn't noticed before. I hear a stirring; young animals come out of the trees to gather at the water. There are birds, squirrels, chipmunks, and a raccoon. Even a young deer on shaky legs bats her eyelashes at me from the edge of the circle. I bend down and see my reflection in the water, lit by the flames of my four colored candles. A ten-year-old girl with red hair, round cheeks, and a freckled nose looks back at me. There is another figure standing behind the girl.

I turn and see the young woman with flowers in her golden ringlets. She is smiling mischievously, everything about her twinkling in the candlelight. Then her image blurs, as if I am watching her through a scrim of smoke or a fall of moonlit water.

Suddenly I am so tired I can't hold my head up.

I lie down on the soft earth and close my eyes.

I wake some time later with a heaviness in my limbs. My head feels fuzzy, and when I open my eyes, the dark forest spins and tilts around me as if I have been turning in circles. So I close my eyes again and curl up into a fetal position, trying to make the nauseating dizziness stop.

After a while, it does. There is only a gentle rocking motion. I open my eyes and see that I am held in the arms of the dark woman I met in the forest once before. She takes a small cloth, dips it into the pool of water, and presses it against my forehead. The scent of lavender is so strong I can taste it, like the pale purple pastilles that my mother gave me on May Day in an oval-shaped purple-flowered tin. I remember collecting lavender as a child, drying it on wax paper in the sun and keeping it in a little purple-and-white flowered cloth box with a mirror inside. When I was upset or unable to sleep, I would open the box and inhale.

The woman strokes my hair and I feel her braid tickling my cheek and her heart beating at her breast. I want to stay here with her forever. I try to say something but no words come out, and I realize I am falling asleep again.

The next time I open my eyes, everything has changed. I am no longer in a forest, but lying on parched ground, surrounded by rocks that resemble the bones of giants in the darkness. There are no sounds of water or trees, no wind, just arid silence.

But there is some water—the same small, round pool. This time, the surface is as thick, black, and still as ink.

I lean over the edge, wanting the smiling child again. Instead I see a white face with eyes that seem to be popping out of their sockets, tangled hair, and sharp incisors, bared like an attacking animal's fangs. I remember the Christmas Eve when I went to check on my mother and sister, armed with my flashlight and phone. I hadn't recognized the Ruby I saw in the mirror that night, either.

I hear laughter like flames crackling. The old woman is standing above me, her lank white hair hanging over her face. Her eyes, black and bottomless as the pool, are the only really visible feature. She is cupping her gnarled hands in front of her chest as if she is holding her own torn-out heart.

This is when I realize that I have made a mistake. I do not want to harness the fates. I do not want power, or to hold Orion, or to bring upon myself the three-fold law.

"The child was you," the crone says. "And so is the shadow in the pool. It can be a part of you or it can consume you. If you step into the water, your spell will be complete."

I WAS STILL HALF ASLEEP when I reached for the ringing phone, trying to silence it. My whole body ached as if I had been beaten. I was surprised that I was not purple with bruises.

When I heard Opal's voice, I knew it was something serious. My mother and sister wrote letters that didn't say much, just asking how I was and reporting on small town news, sending love. They never called.

My father had had a stroke. He was dead.

My wish had come true. I would never have to see his face again, or hear his voice. If I ever returned to the place where I grew up, I would never have to glance over my shoulder, waiting for him to appear with his clenched teeth and his smoldering cigarette. I could finally end the story of the Ruby who existed before Orion. But Orion was gone.

The fear began then. More than any fear I had felt before. Because you can fight back with your nails and fists, by taking legal action, by moving away, by disciplining your mind. But how can you fight back against a malevolent spirit?

MY GRANDFATHER DIES in our house. I am nine years old. I think he had a heart attack or something, but no one talks about it. I don't want to be alone in the house, ever again. At night, sometimes it is cold in an unearthly way, hellishly cold, just in spots of the house, not all over. No one can explain this. Also, my father complains of hearing banging noises in the night. He develops migraines from them. We don't hear the sounds; we think he is just crazy. We do not consider that he is haunted.

These are the emotions I felt coming from my father at the death of his father:

Anger. Pain. Malice. Revenge.

It seemed normal at the time. I didn't have anything else to compare it to.

I KNOW THAT MY FATHER'S FATHER grew up very poor in a house with a dirt floor. His grandmother lived there with them. She mumbled to herself and carried a pin-cushion full of pins with her wherever she went. There were eight people crammed into that tiny house. I saw it once. It gave me shivers, how dirty and small it was. What happened to my grandfather in that house?

I remember that my mother never wanted to leave Opal and me alone with my grandfather. And when my grandmother went out of the room, she'd almost always tell Grandpa, "Behave yourself, now," as if she were saying it to a boy. I never knew what she was talking about.

My grandfather never laid a finger on me or on Opal. He wore overalls all the time and chewed tobacco, the kind that came in a block called a "plug." He'd stand with his back to the corral and make clicking noises with his mouth. My horse, Vixen, would come running from wherever she was. When she saw him, she'd slow down and sneak up behind him. She'd put her head over his shoulder and, very carefully, she'd reach into his front overall pocket with her teeth and take a big bite of that nasty tobacco. Then my grandfather would burst out in this fit of laughter.

My grandfather was a nice man. I was never afraid of him.

What did my grandfather do to my father? What did

my grandfather's parents do to him and what did their parents do to them?

It all gets passed down, on and on. Until it stops.

You can change things with your will, your determination, your strength. You can move away, track down your true love, treat your children differently than you have been treated. But how strong do you have to be to fight a ghost?

I decided I would go home. Not to honor my father but to be with Opal and my mother. And to learn exactly how strong I really was.

home

AS SOON AS I LEFT the airport, my body slammed into a wall of hot, gray air. I had forgotten what this kind of humidity felt like. Sweat sprang out of every pore. Even my eyes felt as if they were perspiring.

I took the shuttle to the rental car and then drove along the curving roads, past cornfields and farms. After a while, a light summer rain fell, tapping the windshield. I was glad for the hypnotic sound of the wipers, back and forth, lulling my brain so I didn't have to think. But that didn't last long.

On one of Isabelle's decks of healing cards were the words, "Whatever is exposed to the light itself becomes light." I wondered what happens to something that is continually, repeatedly, over and over, exposed to darkness.

Before I left, I had told Isabelle about my past and how I had used the potion and worked the spell. She saw my tears then, for the first time, and she rocked me in her arms. From the shelter of her body I sputtered that I thought I had killed my father.

"No, sweetheart. It was a strange coincidence, that's for sure. But Harnessing the Fates doesn't work that literally. It's about accessing your own power."

I said I was afraid the first part of the threefold law would come back to me in the form of my father's ghost.

"But you didn't go into the pool, Ruby. You saw your own crone power but you chose not to enter the dark water. The spell wasn't completed."

I still wasn't sure, but I had to face whatever was coming directly. There were some things I didn't tell Isabelle: that I loved her son, that I had hunted him down, and that part of the reason I had worked the spell was to make him come back to me. I was afraid that the second part of the threefold law would manifest as something having to do with Orion. That was why I had sent him the book I had been writing. If he knew everything, he would be done with me for good and I would no longer have to worry about losing him.

My mother lived in a small brick house in a wooded area at the edge of town. She was going to nursing school and dating a nice, shy widower. My sister lived nearby with her former college boyfriend, whom she had married. She was four months pregnant with their first child. Both my mother and sister looked as if a weight had been physically removed from their shoulders. They stood up straighter and their faces were bright, more youthful-looking than I could remember seeing them in years. I wished I could feel that same relief at the death of my father.

My mother used to say that when she died she would try to come back and visit me as a spirit. She didn't seem worried about my father doing the same thing.

They hugged me and brought me inside, where we ate potato salad and slices of watermelon. My father always insisted on a large, three-course dinner with a meat dish, but ever since we'd left him, we stopped eating that way. Sometimes we skipped the protein altogether. It reminded me of the times when he went away overnight and we'd feel so free, munching on popcorn in front of the television. We still jumped at loud noises, though, on those nights. Maybe we always would.

I told Opal and my mother about England but not about Orion. It was too hard to explain. Now that I was here, the whole thing didn't even seem real. Maybe I had imagined it, like my childhood fantasy about the island of the animals. If I told my family, they'd probably think I had made it up anyway.

You were seeing whom? Orion Woolf? The movie star, the most eligible bachelor of the year, one of the most beautiful people in the world?

My mother and sister talked about their very real, live men, about baby names, painting a mural in the baby's room, about recipes and what they were reading in their book club. They seemed so content. I didn't think I'd ever feel that way. I had been haunted for such a long time, even before there was a real ghost.

AT THE FUNERAL, I PUT MY HAIR in a bun, wore a black linen shift dress, and kept my sunglasses on. I wasn't hiding tears, of course. There were no tears. I was hiding from the corpse in the box.

When we got back that evening, the air was so heavy with moisture I knew it was just a matter of time before the rain came. I sat on the porch with my family, drinking lemonade in tall glasses, listening to the cicadas and waiting for the lightning bugs to turn on. I was waiting for something else, too. When it got dark, I was going to excuse myself and drive to the house where we lived when my father came into my bedroom. It was also the house where he had spent the rest of his life, until he died there, inside its walls.

A car was coming up the drive. Suddenly I saw the trees that lined the road differently, the way I used to when I was a child—each one animated with a different spirit. These trees were all women, and they were swooning, shaking out their green hair, scratching away at the rough bark that enclosed them, restless for rain. The first drops started, then, and the rich scent of the earth rose up. For a moment, it seemed that even the insects were silent.

"Who's that?" Opal said. "Did you invite anyone else over, Mom?"

We all waited as the car pulled to a stop. A man got out and shut the door. From where I sat on the porch swing, I could see the dark curls and the slow spread of the grin across that face.

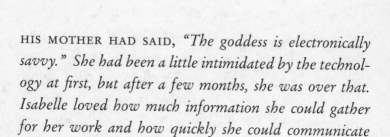

HIS MOTHER HAD SAID, *"The goddess is electronically savvy." She had been a little intimidated by the technology at first, but after a few months, she was over that. Isabelle loved how much information she could gather for her work and how quickly she could communicate with her many sisters around the world.*

He always acted as if this goddess talk was slightly amusing and maybe a little annoying, but really he valued it. Of course, there were the obvious reasons: it was a great way to get women, but that wore off soon enough. It had taught him how to really use his senses and that had helped his acting, he knew. And it had given him a strength and sense of protection he wouldn't have had otherwise. He wondered sometimes if he would have recovered from his injury without having had the belief in magic instilled in him at such an early age. He knew that part of his recovery had to do with his mother and Marie-Therese with her potions, and he was sure it was also because of Ruby in spite of how he had tried to push her away at first. And he had been lucky that finally he could receive it, that the boundaries his first father had were not there to interfere. He wondered if his father and Isabelle would have had a different relationship if he had understood the goddess the way Phillip did.

And then I might never exist, Orion thought.

He no longer felt such resentment for Isabelle and Phillip. After meeting Ruby, he understood better what they had. There was no question that they must be together, no matter what the circumstances.

So why was he here alone in New Zealand, shooting a film about battling a race of beings who, once powerful and full of light, had been driven underground by man to become demons of corruption? Why wasn't she with him? Had he just assumed she wouldn't really want to come? He wasn't used to being in such a serious relationship. Being so vulnerable after what he'd been through with his back and the recovery. Mainly, he'd just been thoughtless, and now here he was, feeling almost as broken without her as when he had been lying on his back after the accident.

The e-mail came a week after he arrived. The goddess is electronically savvy, he thought, when he saw the return address: rubyredmagic@aol.com. It was a brief note telling him that she would be going back to the States because her father had died suddenly. There was also an attachment, and he saw that it was a long one.

At first he thought it was fictional. He knew she was writing something and she had told him she might share it with him at some point when she felt it was ready. But slowly he began to realize that this wasn't fiction at all. Not only the parts about him, but everything—her childhood. He wasn't sure how he knew but he did. That Ruby had not made this up. That she had lived it and survived and it was real.

And there was something else Orion knew then. He would go to her and stand beside her and if there were any demons to fight he would be there to fight them, too. It was one thing to do it in the movies and it was another to do it in real life for someone you loved.

Who but a goddess could have a hand in this? All he had to do was type in a few words and they would reach her in an instant.

the opposite of birth

ORION AND I DROVE DOWN the winding roads, past corn-fields and pastures, toward the last town I had lived with my father. The rain was pouring now. The heat from our bodies fogged up the windows.

"Are you doing all right, Ruby?"

I nodded, looking straight ahead. I felt his eyes on the side of my face, almost as if he were touching me. "How about you?"

"Better now."

"You left the shoot."

"They told me I could have the weekend off. I said my fiancée's father had passed."

I turned to look at him, raising an eyebrow.

"Sorry. I didn't think 'girlfriend' would have the same impact."

"Isabelle told you where I was?"

"I called her after I got the book. I'm sorry I missed the service."

"Thank you for coming."

"She also told me you weren't planning on going back. Will you stay here?"

"No way," I said. "I just needed to take care of this. I don't know where I'm going. Maybe L.A. again."

Orion reached over and put his hand on my thigh. I felt the pressure of his fingers through the thin linen. He wet his lips and cleared his throat like he wanted to say something, but he didn't.

We turned off the highway into the small town. We passed the square with its red brick buildings and flower baskets hanging from the street lamps. Then we drove by the high school, the courthouse, the jail. Everything looked exactly the same as when my mother and I had left.

So did the house, except that the front lawn was overgrown with weeds and there was a FOR SALE sign up. We parked and dashed through the rain up to the back door. It was unlocked.

Orion took my hand and we stepped into the dark

kitchen. The smell of cigarettes was so strong I put my hand up to my face. How had I been able to live like this before? I had hardly noticed it then.

"He died here?" Orion asked.

I nodded.

"Ruby, are you sure you want to do this?"

"I want to spend the night here. In the basement. That's where it happened. If he's going to come back that's where he'd do it."

Orion gripped my hand tighter. I pulled the flashlight out of my purse and we walked through the rooms. The smell of tobacco was everywhere. In the strange light, the flowered wallpaper had a sinister, devouring look.

I jumped so much that it startled Orion. "Bloody hell, Ruby. What?"

It was only my reflection in the large mirror.

The same mirror that had frightened me that Christmas Eve when, armed with Steven's phone and flashlight, I went to check on my mother and sister.

They had smooth, round, pale faces, rounded features and dark, wavy hair. With my red hair, blue eyes, and small features I resembled someone else. Part of the terror I had felt that Christmas Eve, and now, was that I recognized him. Like my father, I was strong, a fighter. Maybe that was why he hadn't been able to get to me the way he did with Opal. But now I'd have to prove that I was stronger than he was.

The basement door creaked open and Orion led me down the narrow stairs into my old bedroom. I had expected my father to have changed everything, made this his poolroom, put in at least one television. Instead, it was just as I had left it. There wasn't even a cigarette smell, just mustiness. My old twin bed was there and my travel posters and Dulac prints of illustrated fairy tales were on the walls. Somehow this calmed me. Maybe my father had been afraid of this room, in some way. Maybe I had haunted him.

Orion sat down on the bed, took my hand and gently pulled me down beside him.

"This was your room?" He looked around.

"I can't stand basements," I said.

"Ruby, I wanted to tell you something. It's the main reason I came here. I mean, besides wanting to be with you for this."

I looked at him, right at him, for the first time, really, since he'd pulled up in my mother's driveway. I didn't know if I could keep myself from crying anymore. He reached up and touched my hair, trying to take out the bobby pins, but he couldn't do it and he cursed softly.

I rolled my eyes and did it for him, shaking my hair

out around my shoulders like a shield. I was still proud, guarded; my tears hadn't come, I had controlled them.

"I want you to come back with me," he said.

Then I do cry; I can't help it. You enfold me in your arms.

"Sometimes the memories are more real than now," I say.

"Tell me a memory," you say. "While it is happening." And then I feel you inside of me and all my body remembers is magic.

It is the opposite of birth. But it is not death. It is the end of separation.

No ghosts visit us that night. It is over. It has begun.

OPAL AND I, DRESSED in our black witch cloaks and hats, went up to the ornately carved wooden door of the yellow Victorian house. If it were not for the nine huge jack-o'-lanterns, we would have been swallowed up by the night; we were that dark in our costumes. Delicious chills tickled my spine and I squeezed Opal's hand.

We knocked.

After a while, the door creaked open, as if by itself. We stepped onto the parquet floor of the entry hall. The house was lit only by candles in pink-and-gold glass holders. The very air had an unearthly glow.

All of a sudden, two old women appeared from

behind an embroidered silk piano shawl that hung in the doorway. They twirled around us, the fringes of their black wraps tickling our skin, the oversized jewels they wore catching the light. Diamonds, rubies, emeralds, sapphires, amethysts twinkling and winking.

"Oh, look, oh, look, our little witches!"

"Don't they look just like us, Ophelia?"

"Yes, yes, Cordelia. Even the hair."

"I was a redhead, girls. And Cordelia was dark, like you, Opal."

"And now you'd never guess! Doesn't age play tricks!"

"Tricks! Trick or treat! Did you say it girls?"

We looked at each other, stunned, and whispered the words. The women reached into invisible pockets and brought out gold-and-silver-wrapped chocolates shaped like bats, cats, moons, and stars. Giggling, they filled our pillowcases until there wasn't any more room.

"Your grandmother lifted tables with her fingertips."

"Your great-great-grandmother was a circus performer. She could lie down across the top of two chairs, even when she was eighty years old."

"Before that your people were gypsies!"

"Oh, we love gypsies!"

"Before that . . ."

"Do you know about fairies?"

"Lots of the magic in your lives."

"All we have to do is ask, girls!"

"Now now you must be off!"

As they whisked us toward the door, I tried to peer into the rest of the house. On either side of the entry, I could see candle-lit rooms full of curvy wood and velvet furniture, lace doilies, books, china dolls, wind-up toys.

It felt as if my sister and I flew on broomsticks down the staircase, giggling like the young girls we sometimes forgot we were.

Later in the evening, we sneaked back to the house and padded around the side in the damp flowerbeds full of the skeletons of rosebushes. Through the lace curtains, we saw the two women sitting at a table stuffing chocolates into their mouths and giggling. With them was a very small person in a pointy black hat, a black house cat as big as a toddler, and a jack-o'-lantern with a carrot nose reciting nursery rhymes.

NOW I KNOW THAT the sisters in the yellow house were another example of the magic that has always surrounded me. I just didn't always see it. But it has been my protection, again and again. I called it to me when I was three and it has remained.

All we have to do is ask.

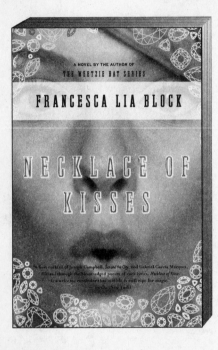